COMING HOME

FAMILY BONDS FOUR

CAROLYNE AARSEN

Misty Ridge Publishing

ONE

What was she doing here?

Garret Bond let the door of Mug Shots fall shut behind him as he caught sight of Larissa Weir in one corner of the coffee shop. She sat across the table from her Uncle Baxter, her hands shaping pictures as she spoke. Her green eyes sparkled with laughter. Her dark hair shimmered in the light from the window beside her.

The green dotted scarf she had draped over her white shirt enhanced the color of her eyes and matched the dangly earrings swinging against her cheek.

He looked at the floor and in spite of his emotions, he had to smile. Her shoes lay on their sides, her bare toes layered over each other.

She always did that. And he always teased her about being an original barefoot hippie.

He tried to rein in his errant heart, disappointed that after all these years she still could make him feel like a foolish, breathless teenager. Could still make him remember, too easily, how much she had meant to him.

He swallowed, his Adam's apple pushing against the knot of his silk tie. He stopped himself from reaching up and straightening it. From brushing the lapels of his suit jacket.

From trying to make himself look presentable in front of the only girl he had ever truly loved.

We were just kids then, he reminded himself. *You're no longer a broke lumber piler working for her dad.*

And Larissa Weir chose her father over you.

"Hey, Tanner, what can I get you?"

A bright, cheerful voice called out and Garret pulled his gaze away from Larissa to the woman standing behind the counter, wiping her hands on a towel, her graying hair partially covered in a pink bandanna, her wide smile like a beacon of welcome light.

Garret resisted the urge to play the mistaken identity game he and his twin brother, Tanner, used to indulge in when they were younger. "I'm Garret," he corrected her, adding a grin.

Kerry Parsons frowned, then her mouth fell open and she pressed a hand to her chest. "Oh, my goodness. It is you. I should have known. I don't think I've ever seen Tanner in a suit and tie." She shook her head, taking a step back as if to get the full picture. "Look at you. All successful looking. How long are you back in town this time?"

"I have plans to stay for a while." And those plans were the reason for his meeting with the man sitting across from Larissa. "Proud to say that Rockyview is now my new home," he said with a grin.

"Or latest home," Kerry said, flipping the towel over her shoulder. "Heard you've been working all over the world."

"I've been here and there," he admitted, trying to keep his focus on her as his Larissa's light laugh tugged at his attention.

"So, now that you're here, I imagine you'll have your usual oversize coffee?" Kerry asked, grabbing a large mug and filling it up even before he could give his order. "Garret?" she prompted when he didn't answer.

Garret gave himself a mental shake, turning back to Kerry. "Of course. Need all the caffeine I can ingest," he replied, pulling his wallet out of his suit jacket.

Kerry took his money, handed him his coffee and, as if sensing the reason for his distraction, gave him a wink along with his change. "Glad to see you back. I know your grand-mother and cousins missed you, not to mention Tanner."

He gave Kerry his full attention as he dropped change in the tip jar. It was dangerous to be seen mooning over his ex in this venue. Facebook and Twitter had nothing on what he and his brother, Tanner, jokingly called The Mug Shots Messaging Service. Anything spoken in the coffee shop traveled around Rockyview quicker than a sneeze.

"I've missed them too," he said. Then he risked another glance at Larissa and the man sitting across from her. Had Larissa been one of the people who missed him?

Garret brushed aside the pointless question, took a steadying breath as he picked up the hot mug of coffee. He walked with measured steps across the wooden floor to the table where Larissa and her uncle sat.

"...so let me know how that works out," Baxter was saying. "We can discuss it later."

Larissa nodded, her hair slipping over her face as she bent her head and scribbled some notes on the papers lying on the table in front of her.

Baxter Lincoln sat back, glancing around as Garret approached.

Garret knew the precise moment Baxter caught his gaze.

His green eyes blinked then his glance flew first to his niece sitting across from him, then to the Rolex strapped to his wrist.

Yes, I'm early, Garret wanted to say. And he guessed

Larissa was supposed to have been gone before Garret had arrived.

The tight smile Garret gave Baxter froze in place when Larissa looked up at her uncle, frowning at his expression. She followed the direction of Baxter's gaze.

As her eyes met his, alarm swept across her beautiful features and her pen clattered to the table.

However, Larissa was truly her father's daughter, so her expression reverted quickly to bland politeness. Her smile reappeared, a shadow of its previous form.

"Hello, Garret. I heard you were back in town," she said, her voice as neutral as her facial expression as she picked up her pen.

"I didn't expect you for another fifteen minutes," Baxter put in, his voice taking on an excessively hearty tone.

Garret gave Larissa a curt nod, acknowledging her greeting, then dragged his gaze away from the woman who had once been the focus of his entire life and turned back to her uncle.

"Thought I'd enjoy Kerry's legendary coffee before our meeting," he said, pleased at how casual his voice came out.

"Of course. That's great," Baxter said, twisting his watch around his wrist. "Glad you could make it." He got up and pulled a chair over to the empty end of their table.

Garret didn't relish the idea of sitting with Larissa, especially when it looked as if she and her uncle were discussing business. But to ignore the gesture would look rude.

Besides, the mug was hot in his hand.

"You go ahead and sit down," Larissa said quietly, gathering up her papers and tapping them on the table. "I should get going anyway."

The coolness of her tone accompanied by her polite smile unsettled him. Especially here in Mug Shots, the place where he and Larissa spent so much time when they were dating. The place he had first told her he loved her.

Then she looked up at him again and he caught the fleeting glow of anger in the depths of her eyes.

His own back stiffened in response as he set his mug on the table.

Why did she have any right to be angry with him? She was the one who refused to come with him ten years ago.

Silence, rife with old emotions, rose up between them.

The fact disappointed and depressed him. He thought he had long moved on. He knew she had. Her silence after he left town told him clearly whom she had chosen over him.

Her father.

She looked away, breaking the connection.

"I've got to talk to Mia about some flowers and then I should get back to the inn," Larissa told her uncle. "Will you be coming there after?"

Baxter shook his head no. "We'll have to finish up tomorrow."

Larissa nodded, then bent over and picked up her briefcase, slipping the papers inside, followed by the laptop she had sitting on the table as well.

Businesswoman, Garret thought, his mind slipping back to the blue jeans, hooded sweatshirts and running shoes Larissa used to favor. Designer blue jeans, mind you, but blue jeans nonetheless.

Now she looked as though she had been transplanted from some Manhattan office tower and plunked into downtown Rockyview.

"Don't forget your shoes," he said, looking down at the pumps lying on the floor.

Her cheeks flushed and without looking at him she slipped her shoes on, which lifted her about two inches higher. She slung her briefcase over her shoulder, picking up her mug and a plate that held the remains of her lunch. As she straightened, her eyes grazed his but this time he saw nothing in their depths.

Which bothered him more than the anger he saw previously.

"Good to see you again, Garret," she said, her voice cool and composed. Then she turned to her uncle who got to his feet. "So I'll see you tomorrow at the inn then."

"I'll be by about eight o'clock," he said.

She nodded and swept past Garret, leaving behind the faintest hint of flowers from her perfume.

The scent brought back another wave of memories. He and Larissa sneaking down the back alleys of Main Street to come here, hoping her father wouldn't catch them. He and Larissa sitting in this very corner at Mug Shots—their spot—sharing a scone, a few laughs. A kiss.

He shook his head as if to clear away the insidious webs of memory. He had to get a grip, he thought. He knew, when he made plans to come back here, that he would run into Larissa from time to time. Rockyview wasn't big enough to avoid her completely.

Baxter got to his feet and shook Garret's hand, as if officially beginning their own meeting. "Good to see you again, Garret. It's been a while."

Garret returned his solid grip, then sat down in the chair Baxter had pulled out for him, settling in. He couldn't help a flutter of anticipation at what would transpire. A few months ago, when Garret was in town for Tanner's wedding, Garret had heard rumblings that Baxter wanted to downsize. Sell off some of his business holdings, one of which was his majority shares in Timberline Mills, the sawmill where Garret used to work, owned by Larissa's father, Jack Weir.

The man who had come between him and Larissa all those

years ago. The man who had fired his mother even earlier than that.

Garret had struggled with his reasons for buying these shares. Holding the majority share in a company Jack Weir owned would give him some control over the man who, at one time, had so much control over his life. The idea was intriguing and, if he were honest, a bit exciting.

When he was younger he had promised himself that the only way he would come back to Rockyview was as an established businessman.

Buying the mill was his chance to prove to himself and to the town that he had arrived.

And Larissa?

He pushed the thought back where it belonged. He didn't care what Larissa thought of him.

"I'm glad we could finally get this meeting together," Garret said, "I'm looking forward to discussing this deal."

Baxter leaned back in his chair, his finger tracing the line of his mustache, now more silver than the dark black it was when Garret worked for Timberline Mills. "So tell me again why a man, educated as a petroleum engineer, wants to buy shares in a sawmill?" His tone was pleasant but Garret sensed an underlying reservation. He guessed it had much to do with Baxter's brother-in-law and partner, Jack Weir. Larissa's father.

Garret took a quick sip of his coffee, searching for the right words.

"My grandmother, as you know, had a heart attack a while back and hinted that she wanted me and my brother and cousins to come back home. And I'd been wanting to for a while." Garret's mind slipped back to the endless evenings in lonely hotel rooms overseas. He'd sensed that something was missing in his life, something he wouldn't find until he came back to the place where his best memories were formed.

When his brother approached him about buying the ranch he was putting up for sale, Garret wasn't financially ready to come back to town. And he'd never been as involved as Tanner in the family ranch. It had bothered him up to think of the ranch moving into other hands. And when Tanner finally sold it, he was broken up. But it all turned out for the best when Tanner ended up marrying the woman who bought it, Sabine Radowski. The girl who used to be known by a horrible nickname —Slobbine Ragowski.

Well, she had certainly moved on from that and now she and Tanner were married.

But seeing Tanner so happy at his wedding, so willing to settle back in Rockyview, made Garret yearn for the same thing.

Knowing Larissa Weir still lived here had nothing to do with it?

Garret dismissed the random thought. Larissa was as much a part of his past as the old football cleats that probably still sat in a box somewhere in Nana Bond's basement on the ranch. He had his own reasons for coming back here.

Larissa's father?

"I suspect you've already talked to the bank about financing?" Baxter asked, a hint of skepticism in his voice as he continued to hold Garret's gaze.

Garret couldn't help but laugh at the doubt threaded through Baxter's voice. "I know you're wondering how someone who started working for you as a lumber piler can afford to buy out your share."

"I admit. I am." Baxter smiled at Garret's blunt comment.

"I lived cheap while I was working," Garret said. "Once I paid my loans back, I was able to save quite a bit of money. I plowed as much as I could into the stock market. I made a good call on some undervalued IPO's after the first big dip in the stock market." Garret leaned back feeling again the exhilaration of watching the value of those penny stocks skyrocket and wondering when to get off the thrill ride. He sold out just a month ago. One month too late to buy Tanner's ranch, but that worked out good in the end for Tanner and the family.

Now he was flush. His decision to wait had changed his life. And given him many more options, one of which was making Baxter this offer. "The bank is willing to work with me based on my assets. Plus, the mill is a good investment with a healthy profit margin." A profit margin that would give him a better return on his investment than his current portfolio. Though he had benefited from the previous jump, in the past few months his money hadn't been doing as well as it could. He had pulled some out to finance his purchase of the shares in the mill, the rest he left, waiting for them to come up again.

"I'm glad financing won't be a problem," Baxter was saying, leaning forward and folding his hands on the table. He paused, looking down at his interlaced fingers, a frown creasing his forehead. He paused and Garret felt a building premonition of dread.

"You look concerned. Is something wrong?" Garret asked.

Baxter blew out his breath, then looked up at Garret. "I don't know how to say this, but I've changed my mind about selling my share in the mill."

Garret dropped back in his chair. "Is this because of my dealings with Jack in the past?"

Or my dealings with Jack's daughter?

When Larissa and Garret started dating, Larissa had been adamant her father not find out. Jack Weir's grand plans for his daughter didn't include her dating a lowly worker at his mill. So he and Larissa had met in secret, which lent an air of clandestine excitement to their relationship. But Jack had found out and the consequences had split him and Larissa apart.

"No, Garret, my change of heart has nothing to do with Jack." Baxter held Garret's gaze, his green eyes, so like Larissa's drilling into his. "I simply changed my mind."

Garret wanted to argue with him, but what could he say? Baxter held all the cards in this deal.

"However, I have another proposition if you're willing to entertain that," Baxter continued. "When my parents died, they willed their businesses to me, Jack and Paula, Larissa's mother. Jack got forty percent of the mill, I got sixty. I also got forty-nine percent share in the Hidden Creek Inn and Paula got fifty-one. I'm willing to sell you my shares in the inn instead."

Garret released his pent up breath, his gaze slipping away from Baxter as he tried to adjust to this huge change in his plans.

"The inn won't net you the same income as the mill would," Baxter continued, "But it's still a decent investment."

"I'm assuming Paula's share of the inn went to her husband when she died?"

"Forty-nine percent did. Two percent went to Larissa." Baxter nodded, understanding why Garret asked that question.

"I don't think I'm interested," he said, knowing what the implications of ownership of the inn would mean.

Larissa worked at the inn. If he bought this property, he would see her every day, not just occasionally as he had anticipated. He was a big boy now, but even the small glimpse he'd had of her today reminded him he was better off getting used to her in small doses.

Besides, he would be a minority shareholder in the business with Jack Weir, with Larissa holding the shares that could tip decisions one way or the other. And he knew she would lean the way she always had. Toward her father.

"I think it's a good opportunity," Baxter continued, "And it will cost you less than the mill."

Garret weighed that factor, letting the idea settle but he kept thinking about working with Larissa.

Your relationship was a long time ago. Get over it.

Garret knew he should. It would be crazy to let an old relationship get in the way of a business opportunity. At the same time, why put himself in an untenable situation?

"I'll think about it," he said, giving Baxter a careful smile.

"Don't think too long. I know there are other people interested," Baxter said.

Garret sensed Baxter's comment was the usual song and dance most sellers used on buyers. Create a sense of urgency so second thoughts go out the window.

"If someone else is interested then that's the way it is." Garret got to his feet, showing Baxter he would not be pushed or bluffed. Then he shook Baxter's hand. "Thanks for your time." He was about to turn when he noticed something black on the floor beside the chair where Larissa sat. He bent over to pick it up.

Larissa's purse.

"Can't believe she left that behind," Baxter said as Garret held it up. "She's always so careful."

Probably in a hurry to get away from me.

"I'm sure she'll figure out she's missing it eventually," Garret said.

"I'll get it to her." Baxter took the purse from Garret. He paused a moment, as if he wanted to say something more, but then pushed his chair under the table. "So let me know in the next couple of days if you're interested in buying the inn." Baxter gave him a quick smile, then headed to the door leading to the patio.

Garret picked up his half-empty mug pulling his thoughts together.

This was not the outcome he had hoped for when he had come here. And he wasn't sure what to do next. Nana would encourage him to pray, as she had when he had visited her a couple of days ago.

She had encouraged him to settle down in Rockyview, as she had so hoped all her grandchildren would. She suggested he turn to God for all the decisions in his life and had given him a Bible to help him on that journey.

But Garret hadn't trusted God since, at age ten, he watched his mother lowered into her grave. Since then, in spite of going to church with his grandparents every Sunday, he had drifted so far from God that praying wasn't part of any of the plans he made.

Garret dragged his hand over his face. Too many decisions to make. One thing he did know, however, he would be cautious about getting too close to Larissa.

OH BROTHER. In her hurry to get away from Garret, Larissa had forgotten her purse. She turned at the next intersection and drove back to Mug Shots.

When she walked in the front door, Garret and her uncle stood at the table. Uncle Baxter was holding her purse and she was just about to call out to him when she heard the tail end of her uncle's conversation.

"...whether or not you're interested in buying the inn."

Uncle Baxter's words were like a shot of ice water through Larissa's veins. She stopped by the cash register, shock rooting her feet to the floor as she grabbed for the counter to steady herself.

What was her uncle talking about? Selling the inn?

And why was he saying that to Garret?

The questions spun through her head as she tried to regain equilibrium. Surely she had heard wrong?

Before she could call out to her uncle, however, he had slipped through the patio door and was out of the building.

She was about to turn to leave, hoping to catch her uncle, when Garret turned and their gazes locked.

His very presence created a flurry of feelings: sorrow, anger, resistance and attraction all beating at her, demanding attention.

As their eyes connected her heart leaped in her chest, stifling her breathing, creating an unwilling sense of anticipation as he walked toward her.

No. She wasn't letting this happen.

"What did my uncle mean?" she blurted out as he reached her side, pushing her errant emotions aside in her need to know what had just happened. "Why did he say he would hear back from you about the inn?" She knew she really didn't have any right to ask, but she needed to know what was going on.

And she needed to keep herself from letting remnants of her old feelings for Garret have any influence in her life.

Garret put his mug in the plastic tub with the other dishes and turned to Larissa, as if weighing what he was about to say.

"He offered to sell me his share of the inn." Garret spoke quietly but his words thundered in her mind.

"Why would he do that? What reason would he have?" Larissa struggled to articulate her rampant thoughts, wishing she didn't sound so foolish in front of the man who had taken up far too much space in her head.

"Because he didn't want to sell me his share of the mill as we had previously arranged."

What was going on? Larissa felt like Alice in Wonderland,

tumbling down the rabbit hole, wondering when she would land. And where.

"I didn't know...Uncle Baxter never said...I had no idea he wanted to sell either," she stammered. Why hadn't her uncle talked to her first? After all, she held a share in the inn. It used to belong to her mother. Surely she had more stake in it than Garret Bond?

"I talked to him about the mill the last time I was in town. I was here to talk to him about that sale when he said he changed his mind and offered me a share in the inn." Garret's calm voice and attitude made her more flustered.

It didn't seem to matter to him that they had once whispered plans about their future. It didn't seem to matter that he was the first man she had ever loved utterly and completely. The first man she had imagined herself marrying.

Even worse, he didn't seem to care that he had walked away from her with her father's money in his pocket and her heart in his hand.

If he did care, he wouldn't be acting as if she were just any girl.

She hoped the chill in her heart reached her eyes but as their gazes met and locked again, she felt the tiniest tremor of awareness. The smallest ripple of older emotions she thought she'd long buried.

She may think Garret didn't matter to her anymore, but as she struggled to hold his gaze she knew she was only fooling herself.

"I'm surprised you would want to buy a business in Rockyview considering you were in such a hurry to leave this place."

When she spoke the words she realized how silly they sounded. She was referring to the many conversations they had, while they were dating, about Garret's desire to leave town and her desire to stay.

Instead it came out sounding like a petty whine from the girl left behind.

"Things change," he said, his ambiguous comment creating a beat of annoyance in her. "Speaking of change," he continued, raising his hand as if reaching out to her. "I was sorry to hear about your mother."

It had been four years since her mother's death, but the pain could still gather and fill her soul with dark sorrow. She pressed her lips together and nodded, acknowledging his condolences. "Thank you for the flowers you sent. That was thoughtful."

"It wasn't enough." His voice was crisp. "Just a small courtesy that couldn't begin to...couldn't start..." He let the words trail off as if they were as insufficient as he thought his flowers were. "Anyhow, I thought of you and your father."

"Thanks again."

A moment of awkward silence followed her reply. She couldn't think of anything to say and, obviously, neither could Garret.

Then his cell phone rang and before he pulled it out of his pocket, he took a step away and tossed off a quick wave.

"I'll see you around then," he said, giving her a polite smile before he lifted the phone to his ear.

"Take care," she said as he walked away.

Her polite words masked other emotions and stifled older questions.

Why didn't you ever call me?

Did you think of me before that?

She pushed the silly questions down into the deep recesses of her mind where they belonged as she waited for the door to fall shut behind Garret.

When she and Garret were dating she was young, foolish

and full of hope and optimism. They were both older now. Wiser.

And both, obviously, had other plans and dreams.

Only now, his plans were causing problems for her. Because she should be the one to buy out her uncle's share of the inn, not Garret.

She couldn't let that happen. She had to find a way to stop her uncle from selling his shares to Garret.

Because there was no way she was working with a man who had betrayed her so badly.

TWO

"Could you at least give me the opportunity to see what the bank will say?" Larissa clutched her cell phone as she strode across the grounds of the Hidden Creek Inn.

She had hoped to talk to her uncle face-to-face when he dropped off her purse, but by the time she got back to the inn, he'd already left it with the front desk. So she had to settle for this phone call.

"Larissa, honey, it's a huge debt to take on. I don't think you want to do that."

Uncle Baxter's soothing tone felt like a patronizing pat on the head. *There, there, little girl. You go play while us men make our plans.*

"Oh, but I do. You know how much the inn means to me." She stopped on the wooden bridge spanning the creek that cut through the grounds of the inn, hating the edge of desperation creeping into her voice. "I had hoped to talk to you myself once I had enough money saved up."

She watched the water of Hidden Creek flow under the

bridge, the light dancing off the waves, appreciating the cool shade of the trees.

She needed a moment to compose herself. To sound like a reasonable businesswoman.

"I had no idea, Larissa. You always seemed so content to manage the place," Uncle Baxter said. "You never gave me any indication of your interest in buying out me or your father."

"I needed time," Larissa hugged herself with her free arm, letting the spray of the creek cool her heated cheeks.

"I talked to your father first, but he said he wasn't sure he wanted to buy me out at this time," Uncle Baxter was saying.

"I know. I talked to him this morning about it as well." Her father, who was in Asia drumming up new markets for the mill, wasn't pleased with this latest development but he had told Larissa that this was not the time for him to make this purchase. He also reminded her that together they owned the controlling share so whoever Uncle Baxter sold to would have to answer to both of them. "So if he won't buy you out, I want you to give me a chance. You know how much I love this inn. I want it to be a bigger part of my life."

And she wanted the authority to make some decisions her father seemed loath to. When her mother willed her a percentage of her share of the inn, Larissa had hoped this would give her some authority to persuade her father to show more interest in the inn her mother loved so much. However, that hadn't happened yet.

"This inn will take over your whole life if you do this," her uncle continued. "Don't you want something else? What about a family?"

Larissa heard the yearning note in her uncle's voice. Her uncle had never married and while he had never voiced regret, of late he seemed to be transferring the hopes and dreams he would have had for his children to her.

"You're the only Weir left," he continued. "The only Lincoln. Don't you want to get married?"

"Of course I do. When the right person comes around."

"You've met many right persons. You just have to learn to give them enough time to pop the question."

Larissa laughed at the dour note in her uncle's voice even as her mind unwillingly slipped back to the person who *had* proposed to her. The first man she had ever loved.

She pushed the thought aside. High school crush. Silly, childish emotions she thought she was over until she saw Garret at Mug Shots.

"Anyhow, I still want a chance to buy the inn," she said. "Could you at least give me that?"

Her uncle released a heavy sigh. "Lucky for you Garret hasn't given me any answer one way or the other, and I hinted that other people might be interested, so yes, I'll give you a chance."

Relief washed over her. "Thanks so much, Uncle Baxter."

"I don't know if you should be thanking me. I don't want that place to take over your life like it did your mother's..." He let the sentence trail off as if giving her a chance to change her mind.

"It is my life," Larissa said.

"That was what I was afraid of." Uncle Baxter's voice grew quiet and then she heard him release a light sigh. "But if that's what you think you want, I'll give you the time. Now I gotta run. There's an employee crisis here at the mill. Talk to you soon."

He hung up and Larissa lowered her hand, breathing in and out, willing her heart to still.

She massaged her temple, feeling suddenly disconnected and untethered. As if the very moorings of her life had been shifted and uprooted.

When her mother died, her father pulled deep into himself, grieving in solitude, leaving Larissa to run the inn and deal with her sorrow on her own. Uncle Baxter had always been more hands-off, content to let his brother-in-law and his niece take care of his sister's inn.

Larissa poured herself, heart and soul, into her work on the inn, determined to maintain her mother's legacy, to keep her mother's memory alive. Though her father inherited a forty-nine percent share, he was never as passionate about the inn as she was. Never as involved.

As a result, the inn had slowly lost money and prestige. It needed a makeover, a partner who was vitally interested and a large injection of cash to pull it out of the hole it had fallen into over the past six years.

Larissa looked around the place, letting memories sift into her soul. Twice a year, after her mother was diagnosed with cancer, Paula would go to Mexico for a month with her friend Lydia to regroup, leaving Larissa in charge of the inn. Larissa loved the responsibility and when her mother came back, tanned and relaxed, they would make plans for the following year. But each year her mother lost more and more energy. In the last six months of her mother's life, when Paula's health was so fragile she couldn't even walk anymore, Larissa would push her around in her wheelchair, stopping here on the bridge to watch the water flow and look over the land surrounding the inn. They would talk of future plans for the inn. Horses and a riding stable. A maze her mother had worked on for a number of years. A wedding arbor.

And every time she would look over at Larissa with an expectant smile as if hoping that Larissa would bring to fruition those very plans.

Larissa knew there were other things that were more important. A new roof. A couple of months ago the Inn had sprung a huge leak in a storm. It had been patched but it needed more work. The windows should be replaced and the carpet. The kitchen needed an upgrade.

But she played along, agreeing with all the romantic dreams her mother spun.

Trouble was, right now, the inn barely held its own. After her mother died, Larissa got to find out just exactly where the inn was financially and it seemed each month it got a little worse. It was at the point that Larissa dreaded her bimonthly meetings with her father and Orest, their bookkeeper and accountant.

Larissa would talk about things she wanted to do to boost the inn's business, Orest would give her the bad news about the state of the books and her father would nix her plans.

Are you sure you want to do this?

Larissa pushed herself away from the bridge and before her second thoughts could gain force, she dialed the number of the bank, asking to be connected to the loan officer who took care of most of the business for the inn.

She *was* sure. The inn held her best memories. It was all she had ever wanted.

Other than Garret.

She pushed the thought aside. She had to focus on the present. The sooner she could get the process to get her loan in place started, the sooner she could stop Garret's plans.

HE SHOULD HAVE JUST SAID no thanks, and moved on.

To what?

Garret swept the question aside as he slammed the door of his car shut. He paused a moment, looking over the property Baxter had offered to sell him four days ago. He looked over the grounds surrounding the inn. The Hidden Creek Inn sat on twelve acres of prime real estate edging the golf course, creating a tiny oasis of peace.

He had let the idea of buying the inn settle in his mind then he had talked to the bank. When he spoke with the real estate agent in town he found out that Rockyview was growing and expanding and each year more tourists came to the area. The inn, with proper management and some financial input, could be a growth opportunity.

It could be a property he could hold on to, then flip and recoup his investment, hopefully with money to spare.

So this morning he decided to see the place again. See if it was as beautiful as he remembered.

The Victorian-style building was built in an L-shape, with a large wooden veranda running along the front and side of the wing. Flowerpots hung from the eaves and nestled against the stairs leading to the main door. The front entrance took up the smaller part of the L and, from what Garret remembered, was where the checkout desk, dining room and kitchen were located. The wing contained the thirty or so rooms that comprised the bulk of the inn's accommodations.

When they were dating, he and Larissa used to sneak over here and hang out in the kitchen of the inn, persuading Emily Dorval to part with some cookies, which they would then take to one of the outlying buildings. There they would talk, laugh and share stolen kisses and plans.

That was years ago, Garret thought. He let the memories rest a moment, then brushed them away. He wasn't here to reminisce. He had business to do.

He shot another glance at his watch, looked over his shoulder, but didn't see Baxter's SUV coming up the long drive to the inn.

He didn't feel like waiting around, so he headed up the flagstone walk to the main entrance of the inn.

Overhanging fir and poplar trees shaded the walk, the wind rustling through their leaves, creating a gentle accompaniment to the murmuring of the creek just beyond the inn.

The same creek that cut through the ranch Garret was born and raised on. The ranch his brother, Tanner, now lived on with his wife, Sabine, and stepdaughter, Olivia.

His mouth lifted in a pensive smile. If he bought this place, then he and his brother would both own land along the creek they had grown up next to. Kind of a nice thought.

As he made his way to the entrance he looked over the building with a more critical eye. Time had not been kind to the Hidden Creek Inn. The exterior needed a new paint job and the trim around the windows was peeling in places.

An older couple stepped out of the entrance, greeting him with a smiling hello and then turned down a side trail branching off the main walk. Garret guessed they were headed to the creek and from there to the walking path that followed it. He and Larissa used to challenge each other to races down the path. She was faster, but he had more endurance and he always won.

He willed away the persistent memories. That was a lifetime ago. He had better get with the present and not get distracted by the past.

He pushed open one of the large wooden doors and stepped inside, pausing as his gaze swept over the entrance. Maple wood wainscoting lined the entrance and above that, the walls were painted a dark blue. The hardwood floor and the large registration desk dominating the entrance matched the wood of the wainscoting.

It was as dark as he remembered it. A lighter paint on the

walls would help. He glanced up at the ceiling. Possibly a skylight.

Then he caught a glimpse of dark hair and his stupid heart did a little stutter as Larissa swept into the room, the full skirt of her pink dress swirling out behind her, her hair bouncing with each step. She clutched a folder in one hand and a phone clamped to her ear in the other.

She frowned, nodded, and spoke a few short words, dropping the folder of papers on the desk, followed by the handset of a telephone. For a moment she glared down at both as if they offended her. Then she finger-combed her hair away from her face in a gesture so familiar it created a stirring in his soul.

She pressed her lips together, drew in a breath and then lifted her head.

When their eyes met there was a moment before recognition dawned, and he saw the desolation in her expression and wondered if the phone call had been the cause. Immediately her face became shuttered and she squeezed out a dry smile.

"Good afternoon, Garret," she said, shuffling the papers in front of her, her voice holding a forced cheeriness. "What can I do for you?"

"Your Uncle Baxter is coming to show me around," he said. "Thought I should at least have a look at the place before I made any decision."

Larissa slipped the papers into a large brown envelope. "Not much has changed about the inn since before...since you were around."

"I didn't know what this part looked like. I was never allowed here," he said.

Coming near the front of the inn meant running the risk of meeting either Larissa's mother or father. So they stayed safely out of sight.

"Like I said, not much has changed," she repeated.

He glanced over at the deserted dining room with its round tables and hoop-backed wooden chairs. Shelves holding antique dishes and knickknacks lined walls covered with rose-printed wallpaper.

"No one eating lunch today?" he asked.

"We're not fully booked," she said, her tone defensive.

"It's the middle of summer. You should be turning people away."

"We should," was all she said, fiddling with the handset of the phone.

She said nothing more and Garret didn't bother pressing the matter, but he was puzzled about the lack of customers, especially at the peak season.

The silence between them lengthened, shifting into awkward territory but Garret wasn't sure what to say next. Another glance at his watch took up a few more seconds.

"I think I'll give your uncle a call. See when he's arriving," Garret said, pulling out his cell phone.

As he paged through his contacts to get Baxter's number, the doors of the inn opened and Larissa's uncle burst into the foyer full of apologies.

"Sorry, about that," he said, flashing Garret a smile. "I had to take a call from Larissa's father." Baxter waggled his fingers at Larissa. "He says hi, by the way. Said he'll call you on Skype tonight."

Larissa responded with a quick smile.

Baxter turned his attention back to Garret, rubbing his hands as if anticipating a speedy sale. "So, where do you want to start?"

Garret sent a quick glance around the lobby, then past the dining room. "How about right here?"

"Sure. Sure. Not hard to see this is the main entrance. Dining room off behind you there," he said with a wave of his hand. "Let's head over there and I can give you a bit more info about the kitchen and—"

The ringing of his cell phone cut him off mid-pitch. He glanced at the call display. He turned to Garret and lifted his hand in apology. "Sorry. Got to deal with this." Baxter angled his chin toward Larissa. "Honey, why don't you show Garret around?"

"I've got to take care of the front desk." Her rapid-fire protest was accompanied with a flip of her hands as if dismissing the notion completely.

"Get Colleen to take over," Baxter said.

"No, really—"

"I don't think—"

Garret and Larissa both stated their objections at the same time, netting a glare from Baxter as he covered the cell phone with his hand.

"Honestly, you two," he snapped. "I don't have time for this. Get over it."

A flush warmed Garret's neck at Baxter's admonition. It was as if time had spun backward and he was again a kid, being reprimanded by Baxter, the boss. He couldn't help a quick glance Larissa's way and from the discomfited look on her face he guessed she felt the same.

And he guessed they both knew exactly what Baxter was telling them to get over.

Baxter sent another frown their way, then stepped inside the office just off the entrance, talking all the while.

An uneasy silence followed his exit and in spite of Baxter's orders, Garret turned to Larissa. "Really, I don't want to trouble you. I can come back another time."

"I doubt Uncle Baxter would be willing to," Larissa said as she picked up the phone. "I'll call Colleen. Once Uncle Baxter is done with his call, he can take over the tour. As you pointed out, we're not exactly all booked up, so I'm not busy."

Garret was surprised at the resentment edging her voice, though it made sense. He knew he felt the same reluctance to spend time with her. But, as Baxter said, maybe they just needed to get over it. Getting this awkward first meeting out of the way would be a step in that direction.

She punched in a number. "Colleen, would you mind covering the front desk for me?" She disconnected the phone, tucked her hair behind her ears and gave Garret a quick look. "I just have to wait for Colleen to come."

As they waited, he noticed her glance at the door, as if hoping her uncle would come and rescue her.

A long, awkward minute later a young girl wearing blue jeans and a button-down shirt, scurried into the room.

"I'm expecting a party at three o'clock," Larissa told the eager-looking young girl. "But I'll easily be back before that."

"Take your time," was Colleen's quick response. "I love running the front desk."

Larissa smiled at that but her smile faded when she turned back to Garret. "Where do you want to start?" she asked.

Garret spread out his hands. "I guess, here."

Larissa angled him a wry look. "Okay. This is the lobby. That's the registration desk." Colleen still stood behind it, straightening the papers piled in one corner, grinning as if she had just won a prize.

Garret frowned at the board behind the desk. "Still using old-fashioned keys?"

"We still have old fashioned doors."

"So what happens if a guest loses a key?" Garret asked.

"We give them a replacement."

"Which means if someone finds the other one then you've got a security problem," Garret said.

Larissa gave him a level look, as if surprised at his observation. "Yes, well, that's another issue I've been trying—" She stopped herself and lifted her hand as if to prevent herself from saying more. "Anyhow, keyless entry is something we are looking into for the future."

She swept past him, trailing a hint of perfume, which Garret followed, feeling a bit like a puppy on a leash.

"This is the dining room," she said, straightening a chair and rearranging the small, square tablecloth, smoothing her hands over it. "We have seating for approximately sixty people though we are approved for events of up to one hundred—"

The large dining room had floor to ceiling arched windows overlooking the patio. Here the decor was lighter, friendlier and standing in the middle of the room, he could envision using this room for banquets or meetings.

"So at most you would have forty people staying or eating here at a time?"

"Or more if people double up, which has happened when the ski hill is open and we're fully booked," she said as she walked toward the kitchen. "Which does happen on occasion."

He ignored her snippy comment as he followed her into the kitchen. She picked up a large knife from a cutting board and put it back on a magnetic strip above it. She straightened a knife block, swept some errant crumbs off the large island and nodded to an unfamiliar woman who had just come out of the pantry off the back corner of the kitchen.

"Do you know how many for dinner?" the woman asked Larissa as she set a bag of flour on the island.

"I'll get a final headcount in an hour. I'm expecting another party at three," Larissa said, picking up a couple of coffee mugs from the counter and setting them by the dishwasher. "Garret, this is Bridget, our head cook. She's been working here since my mom...for the past four years."

Bridget gave him a quick nod, then pulled out a knife and broke open the flour bag. Obviously she had things to do.

"I remember this kitchen as being huge," Garret said as he looked around.

A grill with a six-burner stove took up a whole wall behind Larissa. The island between them stretched out twenty feet. Hanging above the island was a rack from which hung pots and pans and larger utensils. Beside him was a counter with double sinks and next to that was a sanitizer machine. The back wall was taken up by a large refrigerator and shelves holding a variety of canned and dry goods. "Does Emily still work here?"

"She left after my mother died," Larissa said, a puzzling note of anger in her voice.

"That's too bad. She was a great cook." Garret looked again around the kitchen. It had been many years since he had been in this room. Maybe it was just his imagination, but he remembered it as being cleaner. Shinier. Tidier.

"She still is a good cook," Larissa said, striding around the island and back out the door. "She works at an Applebee's in Calgary."

Garret frowned as he caught up to her in the living room. "Why would she want to do that?"

Larissa heaved out a sigh as she pulled open one of the large glass doors leading to the patio. "We had to cut back on our expenses and she said she couldn't work for what we were paying her. So she quit. Then she moved."

Garret frowned, glancing at Larissa's stern profile. "Why did you have to cut back?"

"Income had gone down and expenses had gone up the last eight years." Larissa stepped through the doors on to the patio, waiting for Garret. "So we came to the point where we had to make some hard decisions and Emily was one of them."

Garret wanted to ask her more about her cryptic statement, but decided it could wait.

He turned his attention to the grounds below the patio. He felt disoriented standing here, looking down. He had seen this patio many times, but only from below and often only a glimpse as he and Larissa would run from the parking lot to the back of the inn.

Now he saw what paying guests saw: grassy grounds sweeping down to where the Hidden Creek cut through the property heading toward its juncture with Rockyview, and beyond that, through the opening in the trees, the valley where the town of Rockyview nestled against the mountains encircling the valley, protecting and guarding it.

"I've seen this for so many days of my life, but I never get tired of it," Larissa said quietly, folding her arms over her stomach, her voice softening. "This was my mother's favorite place in the inn."

She sounded more relaxed than she had before and as she stood there, Garret couldn't stop his eyes from stealing in her direction.

Her face held a peace he hadn't seen since he came here. As if being here made her whole. Garret could see why as he turned his attention back to the view. It wasn't new to him. He'd grown up with the mountains of Rockyview Valley and had seen them from all angles and in all seasons. Yet, as he looked them over from this vantage point, he felt a yearning for what he'd had here. Family. Community.

And for a moment, he let the idea of buying this place settle in his mind.

Could he do this? As if drawn by her very presence, his eyes slipped back to Larissa. Could he really work with her and pretend as if they had no history?

He caught a wistful smile as she looked out over the

grounds and his renegade heart quickened. Her face had haunted his thoughts all through college and in the years beyond. Every girl he ever met was compared to her and fell short. He knew he had romanticized her, but at the same time he also knew Larissa held a unique place in his heart.

His first love.

"My father loves coming here, as well." Larissa's voice had grown quiet as she walked to the stone balustrade. She ran her fingers along the top, as if laying her claim to it. "It's the one place he says makes him feel close to my mother. He lost so much when he lost her. He always says that if it wasn't for me, he couldn't get through this."

Garret frowned, wondering why she was telling him all this. It was as if she wanted him to know where her emotions and priorities lay.

She looked at him then, as their gazes meshed, he felt an eerie echo of the past.

Her father was important to her. More important than anyone else.

If Garret did buy this place, big if, he would do well to remember that. Because even spending a little bit of time with Larissa was enough to resurrect old feelings.

He could never let that happen again because apparently nothing in Larissa's life had changed.

THREE

"And that concludes the tour," Larissa said to Garret as she closed the door of the business suite behind her.

She paused a moment, drawing in a steadying breath.

Showing Garret the inn would have been hard enough. Showing him the inn after that disastrous phone call from her accounts manager at the bank made it doubly difficult.

She had been told she didn't have enough collateral to buy the inn. Also, the financial statements of the inn weren't as robust as they could be.

For the past few years she had tried to get a better understanding of the inn's finances. Orest Wilson, their bookkeeper and old friend of the family, had explained the failing situation to Larissa but she wasn't as good with numbers as he was. And he made things seem very complicated. She could never follow his reasoning and was often very thankful he was in charge of the books.

Apparently the bank saw things the same way Orest did and concluded Larissa was not only unable to buy Uncle Baxter's shares of the inn, they did not recommend it.

"Looks like your Uncle Baxter's phone call was more involved than he thought," Garret said, as Larissa turned back to him.

Larissa smoothed her hands over her dress in a self-conscious gesture. She wished she had chosen something a little more professional-looking rather than this flowing dress with its flirty skirt. She was feeling so positive this morning and had dressed accordingly. Now she just felt like a little girl dressed for a party. On top of that she'd had to project a casual and composed demeanor in front of Garret for the past half hour.

"I suppose it was."

Yet another awkward pause followed her statement and Larissa took a quick step past him down the hall. But her heel caught in a fold in the carpet and she stumbled.

She had already righted herself when Garret caught her by the arm to steady her.

The warmth of his firm grip on her arm was as disquieting as his murmured, "Are you okay?"

He was too close to her. She could smell the remnants of his aftershave, the scent of outdoors on his shirt. As she looked up at him, his eyes, steel gray and almost glittering in the dim light of the hallway held her gaze.

He was taller than she remembered, broader and his eyes held an almost world-weary aura. She wondered what he had experienced while he was gone.

Wondered if he ever gave her another thought. He had certainly never written her or tried to call.

And why should he?

He had taken her father's money and run.

She dragged her gaze away from his and pulled her arm free. "I'm fine. I just caught my heel on the carpet."

Garret glanced at the floor and Larissa knew he thought the

same thing she did whenever she walked down this upstairs hall inspecting the rooms.

The carpet needed to be replaced. As did the faucets in the room she just showed him and it seemed every time she checked the rooms another tile was loose, another stain in the carpet couldn't be removed.

For too long the inn had been hobbling along on half-hearted repairs and lackadaisical upkeep. Uncle Baxter and her father claimed there wasn't enough revenue coming in to make major repairs and while they were right, neither seemed inclined to help her find a way to increase it.

"Are you looking at other business opportunities in the area?" Larissa asked, wishing she didn't sound so breathless. For most of the tour she'd struggled to keep a sense of distance both from him and from the dreams that had been dashed by the phone call this morning. As she showed him around, she couldn't help but think of all the things she would do if she had ownership in this place.

She wondered at how their roles had reversed. At one time Garret had been the one without money, without prospects. At least according to her father. Now he could, potentially, become her boss.

"I've checked out a few. Nothing that really jumps out at me."

She kept up a brisk pace as she strode down the hall, but even though he looked like he wasn't rushing, he easily kept up with her.

"So will you be quitting your work as a petroleum engineer?" she asked, hoping she sounded more casual than she felt.

"How did you know what I did?" Garret asked. His voice was pitched low and it sent an unwelcome shiver of remembrance down her back. "Were you keeping tabs on me?"

They were at the top of the stairs now and Larissa laid her

hand on the worn wooden railing, gripping it as if centering herself.

Did he know she periodically went online and checked his Facebook status? Did he know that any mention of his name created a moment of awareness? Did he know that every time she saw Tanner Bond around town her heart flipped over in her chest, then began to race when she realized it wasn't Garret but only his twin brother?

For ten years she had been trying to get over him and she thought she had done exactly that. She'd dated other men, for goodness' sake, and had made her own plans for her life. But when Garret showed up it was as if all the intervening years melted away.

"This is Rockyview," she said, forcing a light laugh but unable to meet his gaze. "One trip to Mug Shots tells me more about our expats than a dozen letters or emails could."

"Of course," he said, conceding her point. Thankfully he didn't press the matter. "But, yes, I won't be working as an engineer if I buy this place, though this wasn't what I imagined myself doing when I decided to come back here."

"So why are you doing this?" She shot him a quick glance disconcerted to see him still looking at her. "Thinking about buying the inn and settling down in Rockyview?"

He lifted his shoulder in a vague shrug. "Your uncle convinced me it was a good investment."

"It doesn't make that much money, you know." She didn't know why she said that. She was supposed to be selling the inn to him.

She didn't want him to buy it. She didn't want anyone to buy it. She wanted it for herself. She wanted to show her father what it could become if he let her take charge of it.

"I think it has a lot of untapped potential," he said.

"I've always thought that."

"You were always pretty connected to this place."

His expression was noncommittal and again, Larissa wished she could feel as disconnected as Garret seemed to be. Throughout the tour of the inn and the property, she had been far too aware of his presence.

They say you never completely forget your first love. You probably never forget your first taste of faithlessness either. Garret had given her both.

"What made you come back to Rockyview?" As soon as she spoke the words, she wished she could take them back. It sounded like she was soliciting for some reference to their past relationship as a reason for his return. "I mean, you could hardly wait to leave it."

Just stop talking already, she thought, mentally smacking herself on the forehead. *You're sounding as if you're stuck in the past.*

"Ever since Nana's heart attack she's been angling to get all the kids back home. And Tanner is in a much better place with Sabine and Olivia, Shannon has decided to stick around. Hailey is back. I felt like I was missing out. Besides, now that I've got more options available to me, I figured this was a good time."

"Options as in..."

"Money."

It was the way he said that single word along with the tilt of his head and the narrowing of his eyes that made the hair on the back of her neck lift. As if he challenged her.

"So you think money gives you more options?" she retorted.

"I don't think it, I know it."

"You do realize you'll be a partner with my father if you take this on," she said, lifting her chin. She could challenge him too. "A minority partner."

"But you have a say as well."

"A whopping two percent," she said, unable to keep the slightly derisive tone out of her voice.

"That two percent makes all the difference, Larissa," Garret gave her a level glance as if testing where her loyalty lay. "If I buy this place and your father and I disagree on which direction to take the inn, your decision will tip the balance. You have more power than you think you do."

She looked at him then, trying to ignore the faint thrum of her heart as what he said settled into her mind. Her Uncle Baxter and her father never disagreed on what was to happen with the inn mostly because her uncle didn't seem to care one way or the other what happened with it and her father was loath to make changes.

Both of which had a negative effect on the inn's business.

But she sensed Garret would have different ideas if he were to buy the inn.

The thought made her uneasy but at the same time created a puzzling sense of anticipation deep within her. Movement. Change.

Working with Garret.

She spun away from him and hurried down the stairs to the main entrance, making sure she didn't fall again. A quick glance through the doors of her office just off the foyer showed her Uncle Baxter sitting at her desk, his back to them, still talking on his phone.

What could he be talking about that took so long?

But, thankfully, her part was done.

With a sense of relief, she turned back to Garret with a bright smile. "So, that's all I can show you. Do you have any more questions?"

Garret slowly shook his head. "Not yet. But I'm sure I'll think of some later on."

"Okay. Then we'll see you when we see you." She gave him

a bright smile and without another word, turned back to the registration desk to relieve Colleen of her duties. As Colleen left, the front doors of the inn flew open and an exuberant group of people burst into the foyer, laughter and chatter following in their wake.

Larissa quickly stepped behind the front desk and pulled up the registration program.

"Hey there, we're the Leusink party." A tall, broad-shouldered young man stepped up to the desk, leaning on its top. "And we're here to party." He added a wink that seemed meant to include her in the joke.

Larissa stifled an inward groan, and put on a professional smile as she clicked on their registration. "I take it you are Les?"

"More or less." He thumped the desk and looked back at the group of six people behind him who released a collective groan.

Old joke, Larissa thought.

She quickly checked them in, took Les's credit card number and gave him his key.

"I hope you enjoy your stay. If there's anything we can do for you to make it more pleasant, please let us know."

Les leaned forward with a smirk and Larissa knew exactly what was coming. "You could come up to Room 207 when you're done working here," he said, tapping his key on the counter.

"I'm sorry. I'll be busy," she said, keeping her polite smile in place, hoping, praying that Les and his group weren't going to cause problems.

For the most part the patrons were polite and respectful, but once in a while the inn got a group requiring extra vigilance. She hoped this group wouldn't be one of them.

"Too busy to come and spend time with me?" Les leaned a

little closer and Larissa stepped back. "We promise not to get too rowdy."

"I think she has other plans." Garret suddenly appeared beside Les. "And I appreciate that you will be respectful of the other patrons of the inn," he said, his voice holding a tone that brooked no argument.

Les appeared to take note both of Garret's height, which topped his by about an inch, and the breadth of Garret's shoulders. His presence seemed to overtake the lobby and Les straightened and stepped back.

"Yeah. Of course. No problem, right, guys?" He glanced over at his friends who all shook their heads as they took their turn collecting their keys.

"Enjoy your stay," Garret said, his smile still intact.

As Les and his group walked away, Larissa felt the apprehension gripping her neck ease away. But at the same time she had to stifle a flicker of resentment. She didn't like Garret coming in to rescue her.

But to say so would make her seem petty. Instead she gave Garret a tight smile. "You seem to know what to do."

"I've had to smooth a few ruffled feathers in my job from time to time," Garret said, his eyes crinkling at the corners as his smile settled into easier lines.

Despite her annoyance with his interference, a subtle undertow emanated between them at the shift in the atmosphere and for a moment Larissa couldn't look away.

"So, tour all done?"

Uncle Baxter's booming voice broke the moment. Her uncle stood in the doorway of her office, a grin on his face as he glanced from Garret to Larissa.

To her dismay, Larissa felt a flush creep up her neck and she quickly averted her eyes, glancing back at the computer as she finished up the booking.

"Yes. I learned a lot," Garret said, pushing away from the counter.

"I know Larissa put the inn's best foot forward. The inn is her baby. She loves it like her mother did." Baxter gave her a quick smile as he joined them. "Sorry I couldn't come. One phone call led to another. I thought I'd be able to help out. But, Garret, do you want to go for lunch?"

"Sorry. I've a few other things to do," Garret said, "So if we're done here, then I'll say goodbye. But I'll be in touch."

"Sure. Sorry I couldn't show you around, but like I said, Larissa is the better person to do that anyway." This netted Larissa another quick smile and then Uncle Baxter was escorting Garret out of the inn.

As the door closed behind them, Larissa sank down on the stool Colleen had just vacated. Her legs felt like they couldn't hold her up anymore.

Dear Lord, she prayed. *What is wrong with me? Why do I still feel this way about someone like him? He's annoying and interfering.*

But she received no divine notification. When Garret had left her all those years ago, she had prayed and cried and shed tears, but hadn't received any answer then either.

Larissa had been a young girl of seventeen, shy, innocent and protected by well-off parents who had their own plans for their only child. Larissa was destined for a proper marriage into a proper family after receiving a proper education.

On that fateful day, however, she was done with school early and, bored, she went to the mill to see her father. She didn't find him. Instead, she found Garret. He was working on the lumber sorter, a tall, gangly boy of nineteen. He had icy gray eyes and long, wavy dark hair. He looked dangerous and frightening.

His piercing gaze seemed to hold hers as he worked and

while it made her uncomfortable, on another level his interest gave her the tiniest thrill.

Larissa was intrigued by the young man with the insolent stare. The next day she found some other reason to go to the mill after school. Garret was working that day as well.

And the next.

On the fourth day he was on his break and he sauntered over and asked her point-blank why she was hanging around the mill.

She didn't know what to say.

Then he asked her out.

She knew her father wouldn't approve so at first she said no. But Garret asked her again. And again. Then, the day before her parents were supposed to leave for another trip to Mexico, she finally accepted.

They arranged to meet in town. Larissa didn't want her father or mother to find out so she nixed the movie Garret wanted to go to and suggested a walk instead.

To her surprise he agreed and seemed to enjoy being with her. At the end of the date, when he brought her back to her car, he asked her out again.

On their third date he kissed her.

On their sixth he asked her if she wanted to be his girlfriend.

They dated for over a year, always being careful, always meeting either at the ranch where he lived or in another town half an hour down the road.

But Garret grew tired of sneaking around and wanted to be more open about their relationship. Larissa tried to explain that her parents wouldn't approve. Especially not her father. If they just waited and got married, her parents would have to accept him once that happened.

Garret wanted to be accepted now. Wanted her parents to know they were a couple now.

They had their first real fight and in the end Garret demanded to know who she loved more. Her father or him. Larissa was reduced to tears. She loved him. Only him. How could he doubt that?

She was so naive, Larissa thought, pushing her tight high heels off her feet, pressing her toes against the cool wood of the floor. Then she really thought Garret's only motive was honor and a desire to be open about their relationship.

So she finally agreed to go and meet her parents.

Larissa easily recalled that day. They walked, hand in hand, to her house.

When her father answered the door, the anger on his expression almost made her back down. However, he invited them in, but didn't call Larissa's mother to join them. Which puzzled her.

They stood in his study, her father behind his desk dominating the space.

In stumbling words Larissa told him she was in love with Garret Bond. That they were starting to make plans. Garret told her father that he loved Larissa. That he would take care of her.

Her father's cold silence was even more frightening than his anger could have been. He finally asked about their plans. How Garret would provide for his daughter. Where they would live.

He grilled them for half an hour. When they left, Garret was shaken and pale. He kissed her goodbye and for a couple of days she heard nothing from either her father or Garret.

Then, one evening, her father called her into his office again. He told her that Garret had only dated her for revenge. That Garret's mother used to work at the mill and had been fired. By him. Garret had never forgiven him and started dating Larissa to get back at him. She didn't believe him.

Then her father told Larissa about the money he had offered to Garret to stay away.

He showed her a check he had made out for ten thousand dollars to Garret Bond. Cashed.

Next thing she heard was Garret had enrolled in college in Vancouver, a thousand miles away. Obviously her father's money had helped pave the way for that particular opportunity.

She never mentioned Garret again and neither did her parents.

The memory still stung, Larissa thought, resting her elbows on the counter, wishing, again, that her mother was still alive. Wishing she had someone who she could talk to about this.

Garret had been a vague shadow, hovering on the periphery of her consciousness for the past ten years, his betrayal creating a distrust of men for many years afterward. She thought she was over him. After all, they were both young. But somehow she had never found anyone who interested her. Anyone who she could give her heart to. Then her mother grew ill and Larissa spent all of her spare time taking care of her. No time for romance.

Now her mother was gone and Garret was back and might be about to become her boss.

A cold finger slid down her spine. What was she going to do about that? She didn't want to have anything to do with him.

And will you manage that? He could end up being your father's newest partner.

She could quit. Find another job. Work somewhere else.

And what about the inn? What about your plans for that?

She pressed her fingers to her temples, making circles with

her fingertips, trying to massage away the confusion and the pressure building behind her forehead.

Then the front door opened and she looked up expectantly. But it was just her uncle. "So, I think that went well," he said with a satisfied smirk. Then he caught Larissa's expression and his smile faded and he strode over to the desk. "Oh, honey. I forgot to ask you if you heard from the bank?"

She waved his question off.

"No. I need to know. Garret seems interested in buying, but if you got approval, you get first crack at this."

Larissa looked down at the papers she had left on the desk before she had shown Garret around the inn. The papers she had spent so much time and effort getting exactly right. All for nothing.

"They turned me down. The loan officer said the financial statements weren't robust enough. Whatever that means."

Uncle Baxter lifted his shoulder in a shrug. "You know yourself the inn has been losing money. That's one of the reasons I wanted to sell my share."

Larissa leaned forward, her hands clasped on the desk in front of her. "We haven't been doing enough here," she said. "We need to fix things up. Put some money back into the place. Look for new business."

Uncle Baxter pulled in a long, deep breath. "I don't have the energy and your father doesn't have the will."

Larissa knew part of her father's reluctance had to do with making changes to a place his beloved wife loved so much. "I think he's too caught in the past," she said looking down at her joined fingers.

Uncle Baxter was quiet a moment before clearing his throat. "Speaking of being caught in the past, how did you and Garret get on?"

Larissa squeezed her hands tighter together. "Fine."

"I shouldn't have snapped at you two, but I was under a bit of a time crunch. I'm feeling pressured right now." He reached over and covered her clasped hands with his. "Forgive me?"

She pooh-poohed his question. "Nothing to forgive. We're fine. It was just a bit awkward, but no, we're fine," she added, patting him on the hand.

Uncle Baxter leveled her a curious glance. "That's good to know, because I'm sure he's buying the inn. He just told me outside."

Larissa could only stare at her uncle. No. This wasn't good. This couldn't happen. She couldn't work with Garret.

But what other option did she have?

FOUR

"Of course you have to buy Hidden Creek Inn," Hailey squealed, clapping her hands in delight, her green eyes glittering in the overhead lights of Nana Bond's dining room. "Shannon and I want to have our wedding there. What do you think, sis?" Hailey asked turning to Shannon. "Maybe he could give us a discount."

Garret grinned at his cousins as he leaned back in his chair. Only he, Shannon, and Hailey had come to the little get-together. Hailey's fiancé, Dan, was away at a conference and his daughter Natasha was staying overnight at a friend's place. Shannon's fiancé, Ben, was working at the hospital. Garret's twin brother, Tanner, and his wife had other obligations as well. Garret had hoped to tell the whole family at once, but he knew whatever he said here would be repeated to the rest of the family, posthaste.

He had waited until Hailey brought out the dessert at the end of their little family dinner before letting loose with his plans. Hailey had almost dropped her plate of squares and cookies, she was so excited but Shannon had looked at him with her steady gaze, as if she knew the deeper implications of what he was doing.

"What is your advice, Nana?" he asked, looking over at his grandmother.

Nana folded her arms, rocking in her chair as if thinking. "You know I'd love more than anything for you to settle down here."

"We could have family get-togethers there," Hailey added.

"The last thing we need is yet another place to get together," Shannon said. "Between the ranch and Nana's oversize house here in town, I think we're covered."

Hailey shrugged. "But still. That would be so cool. Though it could use a bit of sprucing up." Her eyes got big and a smile split her face. "We could have a painting party. Wouldn't that be great?"

"Only you would consider painting fun," Shannon groused. "Besides, Garret would have to run that idea past his partner."

Hailey frowned as if finally realizing what Garret knew Shannon had figured out a few sentences back. "That's right. Larissa Weir's dad owns that place now, doesn't he? Since Mrs. Weir died?"

"Larissa's father and her uncle are equal partners," Garret said, reaching for a cookie. "I would be buying out Baxter Lincoln's share." He didn't tell them about Larissa's two percent share. No sense complicating matters.

"So that means you would be working with Jack Weir?" Shannon asked, her quiet question underlining his own qualms about his business plan.

"To a point. I understand he's left most of the day-to-day running of the inn to his daughter, Larissa, who manages it."

"Would you be able to work with your old girlfriend?" Nana asked.

"Yes. Emphasis on old," Garret mumbled around the cookie he had just taken a bit of. "Almost ten years ago."

"I can't believe she's still single," Nana was saying.

"I heard she was dating Pete Boonstra," Shannon said.

"Property Pete?" Hailey laughed. "That's been over for months."

"That's funny. He came into the hospital the other day and when I asked him about Larissa he made it sound like they were still an item."

"He wishes," Hailey retorted, inspecting a cookie she had taken off the plate. "I'm fairly sure Larissa was the one to break things off. I heard her say something to her friend Alanna about it at Mug Shots when Dan, Natasha, and I were there awhile back." Hailey and her fiancé, Dan, frequently took Dan's daughter, Natasha, out for lunch at Mug Shots which kept them current on local news.

"But now, Garret, when you first came to town I understood you were buying part of the sawmill," Nana said, touching his arm with her hand, corralling the conversation. "I didn't think you were interested in running an inn?"

Garret gratefully pulled his attention away from his cousins' hashing out of the whys and wherefores of Larissa's love life. He was more interested than he should be. "Baxter changed his mind about selling me the mill shares and offered this instead," he said to his nana. "The inn is a good investment. It needs a lot of work, but I think with some improvements and a bit of publicity, business could pick up. I could turn around and sell my share for more than I paid for it if that happens."

"And then what would you do?"

"Baxter said he might be willing to sell his shares in the mill in the future. I wouldn't sell my shares of the inn until that opportunity comes up."

Nana's deliberate nod accompanied by a frown seemed to

say she wanted to understand what he was planning, but wasn't sure she liked it. "So have you prayed about this?" she added.

Her gentle question dove into his soul, laying bare the emptiness of his spiritual life. "No. I haven't."

He wasn't sure he wanted to bother the Lord with his business dealings when he hadn't spoken to Him about any other part of his life.

Nana reached over and laid her hand on his arm. "Then I will," she said quietly. "You know I've always prayed for you? Ever since your mother came to the ranch, rejected by your father, expecting you and your brother, you've been in my thoughts and prayers."

He looked into his grandmother's blue eyes so like his mother's and he nodded. "I know, Nana."

"And I'll continue to pray for you," she said, squeezing his arm like a small benediction.

The thought warmed his heart.

Because he knew, if he bought this inn and had to work with Larissa Weir, he would need many prayers to keep himself from making the same mistake he had when he was younger.

His mother crying in the kitchen after she had gotten fired from working at the mill, Larissa choosing her father over him. And later, letting people take advantage of him on some of his jobs—all of that had taught him one important lesson.

You couldn't depend on other people. You had to take care of yourself.

And when it came to Larissa Weir, he had to be extra careful. Because, somehow, she had managed to maintain her hold of a piece of his heart.

"SO LOOKS to me like the inn has been posting steady losses," Garret said, glancing up from the statements sitting on the table in front of him. "I'm surprised. It seemed to be busy all the time when I lived here."

Larissa nodded, his comment underlining her own concerns about the inn. She could probably recite the profit and loss statement by heart. She and Orest had gone over them extensively before she went to the bank.

Garret drew his lip between his teeth as he rolled up the sleeves of his blue chambray shirt, as if getting ready to do some hard work. "So what do you think needs to change to make the inn stop bleeding red ink?"

"Win the lottery," she said, resting her elbows on the large wooden table of the inn's office.

It had only been a week since Garret had come to the inn, looking to buy it.

In less time than it took to say caveat emptor, Uncle Baxter's share of the inn was now in his hands. Now he was her father's partner and no sooner had the ink dried on the agreement than Garret called a meeting with her. As a result, she and Garret had been sitting in the inn's office since six-thirty a.m., looking over the financial statements. Orest couldn't come though, citing a previous obligation.

It was only seven-thirty a.m. and Larissa was already rethinking the silk shirt, pencil skirt, pantyhose and high heels she had put on when she got up at the ridiculous hour of five a.m. to make it here on time. Most of her morning had been spent deciding what to wear. She had wanted to project a businesslike demeanor.

Impress the new boss.

Instead she fought the urge to push off her shoes, run to the bathroom and strip off the hose.

A movement out of the corner of her eye caught her attention. She shot a quick glance over her shoulder and noticed that Les's group was checking out.

She had been worried about those customers since the first day they came in, but Garret had defused that situation and as a result they had been on their best behavior.

Larissa reluctantly accepted that having a male partner who was involved in the business and who would be here every day was an advantage.

"Lightning striking the inn and collecting insurance would be a more likely scenario," Garret was saying.

"I was kidding," she replied, pulling her attention back to him.

"So was I." He picked up the papers again just as she reached for them. He jerked his hands back as she fought her own reaction. Then clenched her teeth. She had to, like her uncle had counseled her, get over it.

Easier said than done, she thought, wondering why Garret still had such a profound impact on her.

"I had a few ideas but my father never wanted to implement them," Larissa said, aiming for a more casual tone.

Garret leaned back in his chair frowning at the papers he held. "What were some of the things you wanted to do?"

Her thoughts cast back to Garret's reactions to the state of the inn and inwardly cringed again. Though the worn-out appearance of the inn wasn't her fault, she still felt responsible. "Change the locks on the doors, like you suggested. Replace the carpeting, modernize the bathrooms, get new furniture and bedding for the rooms." She had a five-page itemized list of things she wanted to do to bring the inn back to the glory days when her grandfather owned it. "When my mother inherited the inn she didn't want to change it. She had grown up here and loved it the way it was. Then, after a long illness she died, and my father was even more reluctant to change it."

"Because of the cost?"

"He has always balked at the cost. But I think changing things from the way my mom liked them was too hard." She paused, a flicker of sorrow catching her unawares.

Garret acknowledged this with a slow nod of his head. Then, after another moment of quiet, as if honoring her sorrow, he flipped through the sheets and stopped at one. "So we have a dilemma. Draw from the operating loan to fix up the inn and increase our expenses and hope for more business or leave it the way it is and slowly watch the income decrease even more."

"I don't think it's going downhill that quickly," she said, trying not to sound defensive.

"Think what you want," he said with an absent tone as he flipped through the rest of the financial statements, "But from what I see around me and on these papers the income is decreasing exponentially."

"So why did you buy the place?" she snapped. Then wished she hadn't. History with Garret aside, he was now her boss.

"For the potential and the chance to own a business in Rockyview." He put the papers down on the desk. "I think this inn could do much better than it is and I think I'd have to agree with your father. The renovations are further down the list of things to be done first."

She frowned, easily recalling his reaction to the general state of the inn. "You said yourself it needed a major overhaul."

"It does. But let's start with the easy stuff first. Lose the cook. Anyone with a face that sour can't possibly make food taste good. We need to actively seek new business. Are you on the Chamber of Commerce?"

"I am, but haven't had time to attend the meetings."

"That's a place to start. We need to reach out and make connections. Drum up new business."

"That's only half of the battle," Larissa protested. "I have a suggestion box and one of the main comments is the state of the rooms. How old-fashioned they look."

"So we try to draw people in another way and emphasize the food rather than the rooms. As for the bookkeeping, I want us to move into the current century and set up the accounts so that we can view and pay bills online. What is more important, we need to get an external audit done on the books. So that we get a balanced view of the inn's true financial situation."

Larissa felt a moment of confusion. "That makes it look like we don't trust Orest."

"It's not a matter of trust, it's a matter of solid business practices."

"But he's an old friend of my mother," Larissa said in his defense.

"Your mother isn't running the inn anymore and friendship doesn't balance the books."

Larissa blanched at his callous comment but Garret was still talking and not looking at her.

"As for other staff," Garret continued, making a note on the pad of paper in front of him. "I'd like to get Emily Dorval back working for us. I think for now the easiest thing to rectify is the cooking. The rest is fairly superficial stuff that will have to wait until we can increase traffic to the inn."

"Why Emily?"

"She knows the kitchen. And I remember her as a good cook."

"She *was* a good cook. A great cook."

"I sense some hesitation." He dropped his pen on the table and leaned back in his chair, his arms folded over his chest as he rocked back in the chair.

Larissa fingered the edge of the papers she had in front of

her, trying to formulate her thoughts. "I don't know if she'll come back," Larissa said quietly.

"Why not?" Garret prompted.

"We had a bad fight," Larissa admitted rubbing her forehead as if to ease away the memory of that afternoon. "It happened about a month after my mother died. Emily wanted to make substantial changes to the menu. I told her the inn couldn't afford it. She made an obscure comment about the inn's finances. Blamed my mother for not being more careful..." To her shame Larissa's voice broke as she recalled the high emotions of the moment. She was still grieving the loss of her mother and Emily's words seemed callous and uncaring. When Larissa had run the idea of changes in the menu past her father, he was adamantly opposed to spending more money. So Larissa had to go back and tell Emily no.

"A year after she quit I went to go see her," Larissa said. "I had hoped to talk to her, to mend some fences between us, but Emily wasn't working that day and the moment was lost."

"So I have to do some major sweet-talking to get her back."

"And give her a raise and be looking at a large increase in costs none of which we can afford according to the financials."

"We have an operating loan," he said.

"We're fairly deep into it already," Larissa said.

"So we go to the bank and make it bigger. It looks like there's still enough equity in the place to give us some wiggle room."

"We still have to pay it back."

"Part of the challenge." He shoved his hand through his thick hair and shot her a crooked grin.

His expression yanked her so quickly back to the past, it took her breath away. How often, as a young girl, had that very look sent her heart beating just a little faster?

She repressed the faint flutter she felt now, recognizing that

Garret was as good-looking now as he was then. Better-looking, if she were honest.

Then he was just a young man, tall, gangly, his long, dark hair perpetually falling into his wary eyes.

He had filled out, his shoulders had broadened and the unruly hair had been tamed, as had his attitude.

To a point.

"I am sure we can turn this inn around," he said with a note of confidence that encouraged her but, if she were completely honest with herself, nettled her at the same time. "But we have to be willing to take some risks."

"You've never run an inn before," she said allowing a tiny note of asperity to creep into her voice.

He shrugged off her comment. "I've been involved in enough businesses to be able to step back and be analytical about the bigger picture."

She wanted to agree with him, but the niggle of annoyance grew. "An inn is more than a business," she said, looking past him through the window behind him, struggling to keep her voice even. "It becomes a person's home away from home. They come here to rest from a journey they're on or they come here to be away from their ordinary life. It's a place where people trust us to take care of them and that requires more than a good business mind to do properly."

Her voice had risen slightly on her last words and when she was done she realized she had clenched her fists on the table in front of her.

In the silence that followed she faintly heard the plaintive wail of the train's horn sounding through the valley, as if it echoed her own state of mind.

"You have a real heart for this place, don't you," Garret finally said, breaking the quiet.

"It has been in my family for decades and I know it's old

and needs work, but it is still a part of this town's history." She finally glanced away, thankful to see a serious expression on his face. "It has a lot of potential."

"I agree about the potential," Garret said quietly. "I just hope we can agree on how to realize it."

"Do you still think rehiring Emily is the way to go?"

He nodded and Larissa sensed he wasn't wavering on this. She tapped the edges of her statements into a neat pile and picked them up. "So is there anything else we need to talk about?"

"Not for now. I'll take care of Emily and our current cook and let you deal with Orest and the audit. If you could take care of that in the next couple of days, then we can get moving on some other changes."

Larissa released a sigh, wondering what her father would say about the situation.

But then she looked up at Garret and caught his frown, as if he sensed her hesitation.

"Will that be a problem?" he asked.

She wanted to say yes, but in her heart, in spite of her resistance to the idea she knew he was right.

"No. It'll be fine," she said quietly looking away. Then, to her shock and dismay, she felt Garret's hand touch her arm. It was the merest brush of his fingers on her sleeve but it seemed to scorch her skin through the material of her shirt.

She jerked her arm back then chastised herself for her foolish overreaction. And when she saw Garret's eyes harden as he pulled his hand back, she felt even more foolish.

"I wanted to say sorry for my comment about your mother not running the inn anymore," he said. "It was insensitive. I guess I was trying to say that things are different now and I'd like to move on."

Larissa sensed an underlying meaning to his words but as

she held his gaze, she felt the tension between them even more keenly.

"I'd like that too," she said, keeping her own comment purposely ambiguous.

"We'll be working together for a while," he added, his hair falling across his forehead as he dropped his head to one side. "May as well try to get along as best as we can. I mean, the past is past, right?"

She gave another curt nod, and added a casual smile, wishing the action would create a corresponding emotion. She knew he was right, but why did his practical words create a lingering sense of desolation?

FIVE

"Did you have a chance to look over my suggestions?" Emily asked as she slowly walked around the kitchen.

Garret glanced down at the piece of paper he held in his hands and nodded. When he first saw the list of Emily's "suggestions" he had struggled with both the extent and the cost.

It had taken him a lot of sweet-talking and a few promises to get Emily to at least spend a day at the inn and give her suggestions, but Garret knew that the kitchen was the first place they needed to change to turn things around. Feed people well and they'll not only come back, they'll tell their friends.

Emily was key to that. He was pleased that she had at least agreed to come and have a conversation.

"I know it seems like a lot," Emily said, as if he had spoken aloud, "But you said you wanted me to think of quality first so I did. I wanted to do this a few years ago, but Larissa said the money wasn't there."

"Her father didn't think it was," Garret said, feeling the need to defend Larissa.

"There are other reasons," Emily said. Then without bothering to add to her ambiguous statement, she folded her slender arms over her stomach, glancing around the kitchen with the air of a woman who had just come back to find rodents taking up residence in her home. "Anyhow, this place is falling apart."

"It's only been four years since you've been here. Surely it hasn't gotten that bad," Garret said, turning over the paper. Didn't matter how many times he looked at it, the final number still made him gulp.

Keep calm and carry on, he reminded himself. It's an investment in the right part of the inn that will pay off in increased revenue.

That is, if his other plans came together the way he hoped. He'd spent the past few days visiting various members of the Chamber of Commerce, stopping in at local businesses and drinking more coffee than was good for him. All this was in an effort to chase down some ideas he had for boosting business at the inn.

"Shows how much you know about running a kitchen." Emily walked around the butcher-block counter to the stove and leaned over it, looking up. "This fan is so gunked up with grease that we'll need a new one. I doubt the filters have been changed. The refrigerator lost a seal and got mildew. The pots and pans needed replacing when I was still here so that'll need to be done. And don't even get me started on the knives." She shot him a challenging look. "If I come back, I won't cook in a lousy kitchen with substandard equipment."

As he faced down a very determined Emily, Garret felt a niggling of sympathy for Larissa's situation four years ago. He had never seen this side of the cook when he and Larissa were stealing cookies from her cookie jar.

But he swallowed his trepidation, ignoring the dollar signs plunging into a black hole in his mind. "I'd like to go ahead and hire you, but we need to finalize everything with Larissa."

"So this job isn't a certainty?"

"You knew I needed to consult her," Garret said, trying to soothe her with a winning smile.

Emily's eyes narrowed and she planted her hands on her narrow hips. "That girl has always done what her daddy tells her, you know that," she said, her dubious expression tweaking second thoughts in Garret's mind. "I don't want everything changing when daddy comes back."

"Her *daddy* is just a phone call away right now," Garret reminded Emily. "I'm sure if Larissa wants to defer to him, that's all it would take."

Emily replied with a curt nod. "Okay. Then, let's go see what she says."

Garret stood aside to let Emily lead the way. He still had his second thoughts about what Emily wanted to do, but he was the one who wanted her to return. He had to back Emily on what she wanted and hope and pray the chances he took would pay off. Hope that Larissa would agree to what Emily wanted and agree to taking her back.

Garret went ahead of Emily and reached for the door just as she gave him a quick smile. "Always the gentleman, aren't you?"

"Not always," he returned.

"Yes. You were. I always thought Larissa was lucky to have you," she said as she walked to the office window overlooking the grounds. "She shouldn't have let you go." Her tone was careful, as if she knew her words moved into places Garret didn't want to follow.

He didn't. He had come here looking ahead, but it seemed that the past kept coming up behind him and tapping him on the shoulder, reminding him of who he once was.

"It wasn't just her," he muttered, thinking of the last-ditch effort he had made when he came to the house and Larissa stood in the doorway, her father behind her. He knew everything was on the line and he would have preferred to talk to her in private, but Jack wouldn't leave.

Then Jack Weir had told Larissa to close the door. To come to him. Larissa had looked from him to her father.

Then she stepped away from him and shut the door of the house.

She had made her choice, but looking back, despite the pain it had caused him at the time, he couldn't blame her. Not really. He couldn't have begun to give her what she was used to. But he had hoped that his love was enough.

"Maybe not, but I know her father certainly had a heavy hand in her life," Emily continued, her back to him, still looking out the window. "But she was always a good girl. Just let her father tell her what to do too often. Probably what got in the way of you and her getting more serious."

They were serious enough, Garret thought, setting the papers on the desk beside the computer. He had proposed to her. Wanted to move away from Rockyview with her. Start their life away from her managing and intrusive father.

She had been hesitant but then, to his surprise, she had agreed. Oh, the plans they had made. They would move to Vancouver Island. He would get a job as a carpenter. She could find a job as a waitress, or anything else. They would find a small place and live the life they wanted.

Simple. Uncomplicated.

Such a dream world.

Garret banished the memories. Time to move on. Move ahead.

"I should go see what's keeping Larissa," he said. "I'll be right back."

As he closed the office door behind him he saw Orest Wilson standing at the desk chatting with Larissa. She wore her hair loose today, flowing over her shoulders and down her back. Instead of the skirts he'd seen on her the past few times, she wore a loose blouse, blazer and narrow legged pants.

She looked like a cute executive.

Orest laughed at something she said, then gave her a hug. With his arm still over her shoulder they walked to the front door. She said goodbye, waved him off then walked back across the foyer.

When their eyes made contact, her warm, open smile was replaced with a tight, polite one.

It shouldn't bother him, but it did.

When Larissa came into the office Garret noticed the moment Emily saw Larissa. Her eyes widened and then her hand wandered up to her mouth as if to hold back whatever might come out.

"Hello, Emily," Larissa said.

Emily nodded but before she lowered her hand Garret caught the tremble of her lips. "Hello, Larissa. You're looking well." In spite of the tremble, her voice was quiet and reserved.

"Thank you," was Larissa's even response.

Garret knew he had to take charge of the meeting and defuse the tension he sensed was building. He strode to the desk and sat down, glancing from Emily to Larissa who still hovered in the doorway.

"Emily, can I show Larissa the figures you ran past me as well as the new menu you wanted to implement?" he asked, reaching for the papers Emily still held.

Emily pulled her attention back to Garret and shoved the papers across the desk.

"Emily gave me a rough budget and asked if we could go over the menu she was proposing," Garret said, looking at the papers he knew by heart. He waited for Larissa to sit down at the end of the table and then set the papers in front of her. He knew it wasn't a done deal, hiring Emily, but if he made it sound like it was, maybe it would happen.

Larissa took the first sheet and as she read, the frown on her face deepened as her eyes flicked over the columns of figures.

A heavy silence fell in the office and Garret had to force himself not to fill it.

Larissa put the paper down. "You'll need a couple of assistants to do all of this if we hire you. These dishes will require a lot of prep work."

Garret was surprised she could draw that conclusion simply from seeing the recipes Emily had written out. Obviously she knew more about running the kitchen than he had given her credit for.

"I figured that would be part of the deal," Emily said, a faint note of belligerence entering her voice.

"It is." Garret intervened before Larissa could protest.

She shot him an annoyed look, which he simply held, not allowing her frustration to seep into his decisions.

"How will this affect the operating loan?"

"Like I said, we'll have to increase it but you'll still have enough for the day-to-day expenses." He tried to sound reasonable. Tried to ignore the fact that she shouldn't have to dig into an operating loan to run the inn.

Larissa pressed her lips together, scratching her cheek with one manicured fingernail.

"We discussed this," he reminded her and she looked back down at the paper a faint nod of her head was the only response he got.

"Okay, then," she said, folding the papers up. "If that's the direction you want to go, if we hire Emily, I should talk to my father about this."

Garret caught Emily's knowing glance and chose to ignore it.

"I better get going," Emily said, getting to her feet. "I need to get back to Calgary." She glanced over at Garret. "When you know what's going on, call me."

He wanted to run after her, assure her she would get the job but his own second thoughts were underlined when Larissa said she needed to talk to her father.

Larissa didn't give him a second glance as she got up, about to leave as well.

"There's a couple of other things I need to talk to you about," he said before she got to the door.

She stopped, closed the door and leaned back against it.

"So, what do you need to know," she asked.

Now that Emily was gone, the room seemed suddenly close and intimate. The light from the window cast intriguing shadows over her face and enhanced the sheen of her dark hair.

He cleared his throat, trying to focus on what he wanted to talk to her about. "Couple of things. I've been in contact with a friend, Sheila Nixon. She's worked in the hospitality industry for fifteen years and is looking for a change. I'd like you to consider having her run the front desk to help you out."

"That's an unnecessary extra cost," she protested.

"That will pay out in the long run. Besides, like you keep saying, we have an operating loan." He said that so easily, as if he didn't wonder, yet again, what he would do when they hit the end of the loan. The operating loan wasn't endless. And eventually it would have to be repaid.

But he had been watching Larissa the past few days and she was running herself ragged trying to manage the front desk and supervise the running of the inn. If the plans he was slowly putting into place came together, she would be even busier managing.

If.

He dismissed the second thoughts and the niggle of fear at

the uncertainty of his plans. *All part of the process,* he reminded himself. *All part of the challenge.*

"Have you talked to my father about hiring her as well?" Larissa asked.

Garret kept his smile intact, stifling his irritation with her need to run everything past her father. "I don't need to. Not if you agree. You do hold that authority."

She caught one corner of her lip between her teeth as if she wasn't convinced. He wanted to push her to make a decision, but knew he had to move slowly. Especially since she would need to be working with Emily. If she was hired.

"I also noticed Orest was here to pick up the financials," he said, bringing his thoughts back to the matter at hand. "Did you talk to him about the audit? I need to set up an appointment with Albert Grimmon in town and I need to know when it works for him."

Larissa frowned. "I talked to my father about the audit and he said we don't need to do that. He thinks it's like telling Orest we don't trust him."

"What do *you* think?"

"I agree with my father," she said with a frown as if that was a foregone conclusion.

...that girl has always done what her daddy tells her.

Emily's words of only a few moments ago resonated in his mind and raised a surge of annoyance.

He knew he had to tread carefully. If Larissa decided she was running to her father with every decision and if her father was sentimentally clinging to the past as Larissa claimed then any change he wanted to make was doomed. He needed Larissa on board and he needed her to be willing to look ahead and make decisions for the inn separate from her father.

"I told you why we needed that audit done," he said, trying to stay calm. "It's not about not trusting Orest, it's about balance and making sure everything is in order. It's about making sure that the numbers add up."

"It always has been. Orest is the most meticulous book-keeper we've had."

"I heard he's also the only bookkeeper you had," Garret reminded her. "And it's a common business practice that has nothing to do with trust and everything to do with proper management."

Larissa sighed. "I guess I could talk to my father again."

"Or you could make a decision on your own," he said, holding her gaze, fighting his irritation with her. "Larissa, I know you want this inn to succeed. So do I. But I also need to know that you and I can work together. I understand you want to consult your father, but at the same time, I need to know that we are moving ahead with our plans to make this inn success-ful. There are decisions you have the power and authority to make."

She held his gaze a moment, and he could see her uncer-tainty written all over her features. Then her cell phone rang and she glanced at it and gave Garret an apologetic smile.

"It's my dad."

And that's all she needed to say as, once again, she made her choice.

SIX

Larissa sat down in the church pew and eased out a sigh. She was so ready to sit and let the worship service ease away the troubles of the week. Their housekeeper, Helen Rochester, was balking at the extra work Larissa needed done and had insisted on getting help like Emily had. Larissa had consulted with her father and he reluctantly agreed to hire Emily back. At a higher wage.

Larissa's father was calling her every day now requiring constant updates. Orest was balking at getting an external audit saying it wouldn't give them more information than what they had already and it was an unnecessary cost. Something her father agreed with.

And seeing Garret every day was wearing in a way that both bothered and annoyed her.

Please, Lord, help me to get through all of this. Help me to stop worrying about the money. Help me not focus on Garret and the past. Help me not to worry about my future.

The gentle murmur of the conversation of people coming into church counterpointed by the quiet instrumental music of the worship group soothed away some of her worries and concerns.

"Hey, Larissa, haven't seen you in ages." Alanna Lavalle dropped into the pew beside Larissa and set her oversized purse on the floor. "Guess you been busy with Garret and the inn?"

Larissa caught her friend's teasing tone, but let the comment slide. "Lots of changes to deal with."

Alanna brushed back a strand of platinum blond hair that had come loose from the intricate braid crossed over her head. "I heard Emily is back cooking at the inn. How is that for you?"

Of course she would know, Larissa thought. Alanna's chocolate shop was right around the corner from Mug Shots. Alanna had lunch there every day.

Larissa pulled her hands over her face, drew in a slow breath, then leaned sideways to whisper in her friend's ear. "I'm here in church to forget about work. Help me out, girlfriend."

Alanna's cornflower eyes gazed into Larissa's as if searching for the things her friend didn't want to discuss. She sighed and nodded. "Okay. You got it."

"Good. Now tell me what I missed at the last Chamber of Commerce meeting."

Alanna pursed her lips. "You really should start coming yourself."

The same thing Garret had said.

"Just tell me."

"Okay. Jack Sorenson did a presentation on using Facebook and Twitter to expand your business. Dan Morrow talked about the budget. The history book came up again and got tabled again. Renee Albertson from Scrap Happy finally joined. Guess her mother is doing a bit better. And, well..." Alanna stopped there, pulling her lower lip between her teeth. "The rest is boring stuff."

Larissa frowned. "What aren't you telling me? What else happened?"

Alanna scratched her cheek with one long fingernail, still hesitating.

"Just tell me," Larissa urged.

"Okay. Norman Parkhurst wants to add another wing to his hotel. Put in a couple of waterslides, a pool, another hot tub and a climbing wall. All for his guests. Don't know how he gets the money for that." The words came out in a rush, as if Alanna wanted to get them out of the way as quickly as possible.

Larissa felt a clench in her midsection. As if she didn't have enough trouble filling up the inn. Now she had to compete with waterslides and a climbing wall?

Alanna patted Larissa's hand. "You don't need to worry about Norman's plans. They might not go through. His lot might not be big enough so there'll be zoning issues. And even if he did add the wing, his location isn't near as nice as yours."

Larissa knew Norman and also knew he was the brother-in-law of the county councilor and the cousin of the mayor. Lots of connections he could milk to help him ease the building permit through the necessary channels.

She looked back at the front of the church, reminding herself where she was and why she was here. Reminding herself that her business problems were just part of doing what she wanted to. Run the inn.

"I hear Garret has all kinds of plans for the inn," Alanna was saying. "Renee told me that Garret had talked to her about doing a craft retreat at the inn."

Why hadn't Garret talked to her about this?

"I think it's a brilliant idea, especially now that Emily is back," Alanna continued. "Women on a retreat love their food."

"Good food definitely contributes to a good retreat," Larissa agreed, making a note to talk to Garret when she was back at the inn.

Then a movement and the sound of familiar laughter caught her attention and as she turned she felt her pulse step up its rhythm.

Garret stood in the aisle, one hand on the end of the pew, as he chatted with his cousin, Hailey Bond and Hailey's fiancé, Dan Morrow, who were sitting there. A young girl sat on Hailey's lap. Dan's daughter, Natasha.

But Garret's presence was a surprise to her.

Garret had not attended church faithfully. When they were dating it had been a stumbling block. Yet, here he was in church wearing a dark blue suit with a white shirt and a gray-and-blue striped tie, looking every bit the successful businessman.

She thought he was staying at the inn today and supervising the new staff member who had been hired to help Larissa run the front desk. Obviously Garret thought Sheila, the new hire, capable enough to manage for a couple of hours on her own.

And she was, Larissa thought. Sheila had worked in a large chain hotel for fifteen years and apparently was excited to be working in a smaller establishment. Larissa's father had balked at the idea of hiring both Emily and someone new at the front desk but, for some reason unknown to her, changed his mind. Thankfully.

Garret had been around a week and Larissa was already exhausted at being stuck between a rock, Garret, and a hard place, her father.

Thankfully Larissa had been able to see the advantages in only a couple of days. Sheila was capable and had managed to get more done in the few days she was working than Charlotte had in months. She had simplified the check-in procedure by downloading a new program onto the computer and upgrading the two others. No small feat considering how ancient they were. Something else she figured would need to be replaced somewhere along the way.

Then Garret released another laugh, his eyes crinkling up at the corners.

The sight plucked out a memory of Garret standing on the deck of a logging bridge up in Hartley Pass, telling her that if she didn't marry him, he would jump into the raging waters below.

Larissa had almost believed him and had run toward him, pleading not to jump. Then he had grabbed and swung her around, laughing down at her, his eyes crinkling up in the same way.

Just kidding, he had said. *I'm not the kind to make needless sacrifices.*

He was certainly right on that score.

"He is as good-looking as he ever was," Alanna said with a gentle sigh.

"Who is?" Larissa asked, turning back to her friend, pretending ignorance of her subject.

Alanna gave Larissa a knowing look. "You know exactly who I'm talking about. Don't tell me he doesn't make your heart go all pitty-pat?"

"Pitty-pat? What are you? Four?" Larissa flashed Alanna a tight grin, trying to shift the conversation to a lighter level. Her good friend's gushing over Garret was not helping. "Besides, I thought you had a thing for someone else whose name you won't give me."

"Thump, thump. Boom, boom," Alanna said, glancing back at Garret and ignoring Larissa's decoy. "Myself, I prefer pitty-pat. It's not too dramatic and a little bit silly—which is just the way you used to act around him."

"What I prefer is that you tell me about that new product you were talking about bringing in," Larissa said, shifting to something else to distract her friend. "Wasn't it something about chocolate hearts?"

"So we're allowed to talk about my business in church but not yours?" Alanna settled back in the pew and released a sigh.

"That's right," Larissa said, hoping Alanna took the hint and let her move on.

"The hearts are huge. And they're all chocolate. But the coolest thing is that they're hollow and filled with other chocolate hearts."

Larissa tried to pay attention, she truly did. But as Alanna spoke Larissa caught a glimpse of a dark blue suit and she realized, to her intense dismay, that Garret and his nana had taken a seat two rows in front of her and to her right. She could see him, but he couldn't see her.

Seriously? Couldn't she get even a single break from the man?

She turned her attention back to Alanna who had finished talking and was looking at her with sympathy, realizing Larissa had completely missed out on the chocolate heart update.

"You still like him, don't you?" she whispered, leaning closer to Larissa.

"Honestly, Alanna, it's been years," she whispered back. "The only thing I've gotten from him in all that time was a bouquet of flowers when my mother died. Garret Bond has moved on." She clamped her lips together, stemming the angry tide of emotion negating her words.

Alanna's knowing look only served to underline a fact slowly making itself known to Larissa.

She hadn't ever truly gotten over Garret. He would always hold a piece of her heart.

She turned ahead, trying to ignore both Alanna and the man in her peripheral vision. A man she was far too aware of.

A man she didn't dare trust with her heart.

"...DO nothing out of selfish ambition or vain conceit. Hard words for us to absorb, especially because so many of the things we do in life, we do for ourselves."

The minister's words settled into Garret's soul, creating a discomfort he didn't want to analyze.

Do nothing out of selfish ambition.

Wasn't his buying the inn selfish?

It's business, he reminded himself.

Business that you're thinking of getting rid of as soon as you can.

Only after I make it profitable, which will benefit Larissa in the long run.

Garret folded his arms over his chest, trying to still the warring thoughts, letting the minister's words flow past him. He shouldn't have come this morning anyway. It was Larissa's weekend off. He had just hired Sheila and he should have stayed around to make sure everything was going okay.

However, he had promised his nana he would try to come to church and if he were completely honest, part of him wanted to come for another reason.

The reason being the woman sitting behind him and about fifteen feet over. The woman he'd been aware of ever since he sat down.

He shifted his weight, which netted him a frown from his nana. He gave her a quick smile of apology, then bent forward, resting his elbows on his knees, trying to shut thoughts of Larissa out of his mind. This, however, was growing harder and harder. Every day he spent with her wore at the barriers he'd put around his heart. Every time he saw her face, heard her voice it was as if time shifted backward.

He knew he had to keep his focus on the reason he came here. Fix up the inn. Sell it. Buy the mill when it came available. And he knew it would. From the chit chat around town Baxter was still talking about selling it eventually. Well, Garret was willing to stick around for eventually.

Selfish ambition.

The words resonated in his mind and he tried to dismiss them. Was trying to make your way in life selfish?

Depends on your reasons.

Garret shot a glance in the other direction to where his brother sat with his wife and Sabine's little girl, Olivia. Three years ago his brother was a broken, hurting man, rejecting God and family, trying to get over the death of his daughter and wife.

Now he looked peaceful. Settled. The ranch was doing okay. Not making great money, but doing okay. Tanner seemed happy with that.

Garret couldn't help flashing back to the memory of his mother's tears when she got fired from the mill. The helplessness he felt watching her, knowing he couldn't do anything about it. He remembered all too well the humiliation of wearing patched jeans to school. The lack of money that seemed a constant worry.

You've got to take care of yourself.

Garret sighed again, sitting up, ignoring his nana's admonishing glance at his restlessness. He'd seen that glance enough as a child. He could never sit still. Always had to be on the go. After his mother died, that busyness morphed into a need to find a way to make somebody pay for what happened to his mother.

That somebody had been Jack Weir.

When he first met Larissa he thought he had figured out how to accomplish this. He had thought that by dating her he could get to Jack. Instead, Larissa got to him and had softened his hard heart. Had given him a purpose at least for a while.

Now he could sense her presence as real as a touch.

He leaned forward again, this time directing his focus on the minister, trying to shift his attention away from Larissa.

"...in the end the reality is, as the bumper sticker says, he who dies with the most toys, still dies. Doesn't matter what we gain in our life, it will all turn to dust. Our purpose in life is not to amass, to collect, but to find our way to serve the Lord in all our actions."

The pastor's words were like a twist of a knife. Ever since Garret decided that money gave a person power, he promised himself that someday he would have that power too. But what the minister was saying shed a harsh light of truth on his actions, revealing them for the shallow plans they were.

So what should he do instead? What was the solution?

Garret blanked out both his questions and the minister's words instead, concentrating on his next step with the inn. He'd heard that Pete Boonstra was chairman of the tenth anniversary celebration of the real estate company he worked for and that he had booked The Pines for his banquet and awards dinner.

But yesterday, at Mug Shots, he'd heard that The Pines had suffered major water damage when some main pipes burst and Garret also knew their kitchen was out of commission. So of necessity they had canceled all engagements for a month.

Garret also heard that Pete was now desperately looking for another place to hold the celebration, which was supposed to happen in three weeks. It had been a built-in opportunity to get more business for the inn and Garret had taken advantage of it.

He reached for his cell phone to check it, then glanced at his nana and caught himself.

You don't need to do this in church. He lowered his hand just as the minister announced the closing song. With a start he realized that church was winding down.

He got to his feet and joined in on the song. When the last note was sounded, he stopped himself from looking back to where Larissa sat with her friend Alanna. He resolutely turned his back on her, hoping to leave another way. Coming to church today had been a mistake. He had to keep his personal life separate from his business.

Which was hard enough to do in a town like Rockyview. His phone buzzed, thankfully the service was over, and he pulled it out.

He grinned. Pete had agreed to come tomorrow to talk to him. But before he could tap out a reply, his nana caught him by the arm.

"There's someone I'd like you to meet," she said, pulling him back in the direction he was trying to escape. "Stay here and I'll be right back."

So he did, but his change in position put him face-to-face with Larissa who was walking out of her pew.

"Good morning, Garret," she said, her voice quiet, even. Like it always was around him. "Good to see you here."

Her last comment came out with a hint of a question embedded in it. As if she was wondering why he was here this morning.

"Sheila had things under control at the inn," he said, feeling as if he had to justify his presence. "So I figured I could leave."

"That's why we hired her," Larissa said. "So I'm glad that you could come this morning too."

"Nana Bond wanted me to come," he said.

Her expression shifted a bit at that. "I see."

Only two words but he sensed disappointment in them.

He remembered how she had always asked him to come to church with her when they were dating. How he didn't want to because that would mean seeing Jack Weir. And it would mean coming into contact with a God he had always believed had taken his mother. He didn't trust God. At least he hadn't then. However, of late a new emptiness had entered his soul. So he had come to church, hoping, wondering if that would fill it.

"But it was a good service," he added. This was true enough. He had enjoyed parts of it. "It was good to feel part of...part of the community."

"It's a good community," she said quietly.

"Speaking of, I set up a meeting with Pete Boonstra tomorrow, first thing in the morning at the inn," he said. "I'm trying to get him to consider the inn for his real estate shindig."

Alanna frowned, poking Larissa in the back. "How come he gets to talk business in church, but I don't?"

"Just leave it be," Larissa said to her friend. Then she turned back to Garret. "What time?"

"I can call you later," he said, feeling suddenly foolish after Alanna's comment. He felt like a man playing a game without knowing the rules.

"No. Just tell me now," she said.

"He wants to meet early. Before he opens up his business, so he'll be there at seven-thirty."

"I'll be there," she said. "Anything else I need to know?"

He was about to say more when a woman came up behind Larissa and caught her by the shoulder to get her attention. "Hey, sweetie," the woman said. "Good to see you. How's things at the inn with your new boss?"

Larissa turned to the woman. "Fine, Daphne," she said, By the way—"

"I hear Garret is the new boss," Daphne said not letting

Larissa finish. "How's that working out for you? Not tempted to rekindle the old romance? I know it took you a while to get over him."

A flush crept up Larissa's neck but before she could correct her, Daphne turned to Garret. "Hey, Tanner. Like the suit. Never seen that on you before. Sabine talk you into it?"

"Daphne, this is Garret," Larissa said, lifting a hand in his direction.

Daphne frowned, then she clapped her hand over her mouth, but it was too late. The words had flown out and could not be retrieved.

"Oh. My. I am...I can't believe...I'm so sorry." Daphne lowered her hand, her cheeks flaming as her gaze flicked from Larissa to Garret, then locked on Larissa. "Honest mistake, right? I mean, they look so much alike and Garret never went to church..." Daphne shook her head, looking down. "And I'm stopping now."

"You might want to join On and On Anon," Alanna joked. "The support group I've started for compulsive talkers."

Daphne released a nervous laugh, shot Garret another quick glance, then drew away. "I'll catch up later," she mumbled.

Larissa looked like she was about to say something more but was saved when Garret's nana hustled over. "So, Garret, I want you to meet Sophie Brouwer. She's Ben's mom." An older woman stood behind Nana Bond, her white hair permed to an inch of its life. She wore a hot pink dress and a cheerful grin.

"If all goes according to plan, I'll also be your cousin's mother-in-law now that Ben and Shannon are engaged," Sophie Brouwer was saying, holding out her hand to Garret.

Garret shook her tiny hand, surprised at the strength of her handshake. "Congratulations. I haven't met Ben yet, but I've heard good things about him."

"Of course you have. Your nana is as in love with him as I am with Shannon," Sophie said, her smile fairly taking over her face. "We are so blessed. And we're neighbors too."

In the ensuing chatter, Larissa and Alanna had exited the pew, walking arm in arm down the aisle, their heads together, just like they always did in school.

Probably laughing, he thought. *Probably talking about what just happened just like they always did.*

He turned back to Sophie, part of his attention on her chitchat.

But another part of his mind couldn't forget Daphne's puzzling comment.

"...it took you a while to get over him."

What did she mean by that? And would he find out?

SEVEN

"I'd love to hold our banquet here at the inn, Garret, but we're figuring on about thirty people staying overnight," Pete Boonstra said, tapping his pen on the table tucked into one corner of the inn's office. "I'm not sure you can accommodate us."

"We have thirty rooms," Garret said, leaning back in his chair, trying not to get pulled into the trepidation in Pete's voice.

Pete's sigh seemed to reverberate around the room. "Yeah and about half of them need work."

Before Garret could respond to that the door of the office opened and Larissa slipped in. "Sorry I'm late," she said with an apologetic smile. "Had to help Emily with a supply list." She glanced at Garret and for a moment their gazes held, creating a surprising awareness, sparked yesterday at church, and wavered between them.

I know it took you a while to get over him.

All day yesterday Daphne's comment had stayed in his mind, raising questions he wasn't sure he wanted answered.

He had come here to build a future, not cling to a past

Larissa was a part of. The emotions she created were just an echo of old unresolved feelings. Nothing more.

Yet, as she sat down across from him, he had a sense of homecoming. Of rightness.

He brushed the feelings aside as leftover emotions from a past he was trying to leave behind.

"No problem," he said, his voice brisk and professional. "We had just got started."

A frown creased Larissa's forehead, as she wondered at his tone, but then she turned to Pete, holding out her hand. "Nice to see you again, Pete."

Pete's smile grew as he stood and he grasped Larissa's hand with both of his in, what looked to Garret, too friendly of a display. "Great to be here. You're looking as beautiful as always."

Garret resisted the urge to roll his eyes at the obvious flattery.

"I'm sorry you missed the last Chamber of Commerce meeting," Pete continued, pulling out a chair for Larissa, making Garret suddenly feel gauche and inconsiderate. He should have done that. He should have stood when Larissa came into the room. His nana taught him better than that.

But being around Larissa put him on the defensive and seemed to make him forget his manners.

So he gave her a quick smile, by way of apology.

Her answering smile was supposed to simply grant him absolution, but it settled into his soul creating an unwelcome reaction.

"I heard you're thinking of the inn to hold your mini-conference," Larissa was saying, pulling her chair just a bit closer to the table, resting her folded hands on its scarred and nicked surface.

"Thinking of it," Pete said. "Garret has been selling me on the various aspects of having it here."

"It's a great location. Peaceful grounds, idyllic setting," Larissa said in reply.

Garret tried not to jump in, letting Larissa's soothing voice do its job.

The inn really needed to get this mini-conference. Pete not only worked as a real estate agent, but he was also a major player in the Chamber of Commerce's newest venture promoting various businesses of Rockyview. Garret needed him pushing the inn.

"It is all that," Pete was saying, "But I'm not sure the people would want to stay here."

"Why not?" Garret asked.

"I don't think the decor has been changed since the '60s," he said.

"So it's retro. All the rage," Garret said with a forced laugh, avoiding Larissa's gaze, remembering the conversation they had in this very place about this very thing.

"Shabby retro, more like," Pete said.

"We've got a fantastic menu," Larissa put in. "And Emily is cooking for us again. She's expanded it and you can't argue with the prices."

Fire sale prices, Garret thought, but for now the lower prices were a way of bringing in new customers. And hopefully generating that elusive word of mouth that could attract more customers.

"I heard that Emily was back and that the food is better," Pete said. "It was one of the reasons I was willing to have this meeting."

Score one for his decision, Garret thought, sitting up. He had seen the evidence himself. The past week the number of people coming to the inn had increased every day, taking advantage of the inn's "Buy one meal, Get one free" campaign and raving about the new menu and the food. In fact, last night people had to line up and wait their turn to eat. Larissa had fussed about making people wait, but Garret was secretly pleased. A line outside a restaurant was never bad publicity.

"People won't remember the food when they have to sleep in a dingy room," Pete continued.

"So what didn't you like about the rooms?" Larissa asked, leaning just a bit forward, her smile engaging, welcoming.

Garret frowned. She wasn't flirting with Pete was she?

And why should he care if she was?

"The rooms seemed dark," Pete was saying. "Dull. Some of the bedspreads are still those old, shiny ones my grandmother has on her bed and the pictures on the wall..." Pete stopped, looking apologetic. "I'm sorry, Larissa, but you really should look at doing some renos on the place. Sprucing it up a bit. Making it look more modern."

"If we did, would that make a difference for your staying here?" Larissa asked.

"Well, it would probably help. Though I'm not sure how you could do that before the conference."

Larissa nodded, then turned back to Garret as if to tell him that the ball was in his court now.

He had to smile at her deft shifting of the responsibility and he appreciated the lack of a knowing smirk.

The thought of spending more money and possibly closing the inn while they made the changes Pete wanted gave him a clench in his stomach. And how much should they do?

After outfitting and fixing up the kitchen, the inn's books were down to the last few dollars of the operating loan. He hadn't pulled a wage since he started here and if they were to do more work, he'd have to dig into the money he was using to live on to finance the extra outlay. And how much would it take? The inn was still bleeding red ink and turning a profit was so far down the road, it looked like a mirage.

He'd been working every extra hour he could mowing lawns and trying to bring some order back to overgrown flowerbeds. According to Larissa they had to cut back on maintenance two years ago and the place showed it.

Regrets twisted his stomach. He stood to lose what had taken him so long to get together. Maybe he should just sell his share of the inn.

Don't be a wimp. This is just another challenge. You've dealt with blown out wells in Dubai and last-minute number-crunching to save a project. The dining room is already pulling in extra money, things will change.

He knew he only had to hang on to this place long enough to maybe not show a profit, but the potential of a profit for any new buyer to be interested in his share.

"Okay, how about this," he said to Pete, fighting down his own misgivings and concerns. "You know we have the space and the ability to handle your conference," he said projecting a confidence he didn't feel. "I also know you'll have a hard time finding a place in town on such short notice that can offer what we can and I know you want to hold the event in Rockyview. Give us two weeks to do some work on the place, then come back again. If you don't like what you see, you've not lost anything."

Pete grimaced. "I don't know."

"Do you have another venue lined up?"

Pete's grimace deepened. "No."

"So you have no idea where you're holding a conference people have already booked for?"

"You don't need to rub it in," Pete said with a nervous

laugh. "I've been talking to people in Cranbrook and I have a possible there…"

"You sure you want to take your conference so far from town? I know you've scheduled some events here in Rockyview. I also know you want to bring the people out to Coal Creek Estates, your little crown jewel of real estate up by the ski hill."

"Yeah. I do." Pete ran his hand over his head, shooting Larissa a glance as if hoping she would help him out. Somehow.

But she was looking at Garret, a hint of a smile playing around her lips accompanied by a twinkle in her eyes and a dimple in one cheek. Her hair slipped over one flushed cheek and caught the sun slanting through the windows.

He couldn't look away and didn't want to. The silence in the room seemed to deepen as his pulse stepped up just a bit.

Her lips parted, and his pulse increased.

This was crazy, he thought, knowing he should look away, but unable to. He had his plans and Larissa wasn't a part of them.

She was. Once.

That was too long ago. He had changed too much and she had changed too little.

He pulled his attention back to Pete.

"Tell you what I'll do for you, Pete," he said, leaning forward, bringing his attention back to the matter at hand. "If you find another place and you need to put down a deposit, go ahead. But I want you to come back here and check this place out in two weeks before you make your final decision. If it meets your approval, then I'll take the deposit you gave the other hotel off the price."

He swallowed down the panic his rash promise created. More money down the drain. More red ink bleeding on to the inn's register.

Money is just a tool.

He learned that watching his stocks do their roller-coaster dive and climb. However, he had never forgotten counting every penny when he was younger and often more than once.

In his peripheral vision he caught Larissa's concerned frown, but he kept his attention on Pete, afraid his fish might come off the hook if he didn't maintain eye contact.

Pete bit his lip, ran his hand over his face then, after what seemed like eons, nodded. "Okay. You got it. I'll be back in two weeks and if I like what you've done, then we'll talk."

Not the firm commitment Garret had hoped for but it was a start.

Pete got to his feet and Garret stood and held out his hand. "Thanks for coming by. We can still book the test meal if you want."

Pete waved off the offer. "I've already eaten here. The food is really good. Excellent, in fact." He glanced from Garret to Larissa. "I wouldn't mind a tour of the grounds. I've never walked over them before."

Garret tried to keep the smile on his face thinking of the long grass and the weeds encroaching on the pond. He hadn't had a chance to get to them yet. He knew the land surrounding the inn wasn't what it used to be, but hopefully the space and beauty of the place would speak for itself. And hopefully Pete would see the potential in what Garret had already accomplished.

"Would you be willing to do that, Larissa?" Garret asked.

"Sorry. Would you mind doing it? I'm a bit swamped right now," she said with an apologetic smile, waving him off.

Why did her choice to avoid Pete make him feel a bit better?

Because you're a typical guy, Garret thought, giving himself a mental shake. *You're not dating her, but you don't like the idea of someone else being with her.*

Pete looked as disappointed as Garret was relieved, but he gave Larissa a quick smile while leaving the office.

"I really appreciate you giving us a chance," Garret said as they walked through the lobby.

"I'm interested to see what you come up with," Pete said, shooting another glance over his shoulder at the office as if hoping Larissa would change her mind.

Garret opened the door for him and Pete stepped outside.

"What do you want to see first?" Garret asked, his tone suddenly brisk and businesslike. He was here to sell.

Pete shifted his briefcase from one hand to the other in a nervous gesture. "You may as well know I didn't really want a tour of the grounds," Pete said with a wry grin. "At least, not with you. So we don't need to go through the charade."

Relief shimmered through Garret. One less thing he would have to try to "sell" to Pete.

"You would have preferred Larissa?" Garret tried to keep his tone light. As if it didn't matter that Pete and Larissa had dated at one time.

"Yeah."

"I understood you guys were an item once."

Pete angled him a wry glance. "Why do you want to know?"

Garret lifted his shoulder in an offhand gesture. "Just making conversation."

"I don't think you are. I know your history. I know you used to date her," Pete said, his eyes steady on Garret. "And from the way you were looking at her this morning, I get the feeling she still means a lot to you."

Garret's first reaction was to deny whatever Pete said. His

second was embarrassment that his feelings had been that apparent.

If they had been obvious to Pete, what had Larissa seen?

"I don't think she noticed," Pete said, as if he could read Garret's thoughts. "And I was watching her a lot."

"I know," Garret replied.

Pete tweaked out a dry smile edged with regret. "She was never that interested in me. I think she dated me to try things out. I always got the sense her heart was already taken. Or still taken," he said.

Garret didn't want his own heart to quicken at what Pete said. Didn't want to feel that spark of hope rekindled. But Pete's comment came too close to what Daphne had said yesterday.

Had Larissa really missed him? Had it really taken her time to get over him? He shook the feeling off. He had come here with a plan and he couldn't afford to let Larissa distract him from that.

"So, back to the conference," Garret said, "I'm looking forward to seeing you in two weeks."

"I'll let you know what happens," was all Pete said. "We'll stay in touch." Then he turned and walked down the path to the parking lot.

Before he went back into the inn he glanced over his shoulder again at the property and a comment Larissa had made rose up, adjusting his perspective.

People come here to rest from a journey they're on.

He thought of all the places he'd stayed during his business trips. Every time he'd come into a hotel room or inn, the first thing he would do was drop his suitcase to the floor and walk to the window to check out the view. Usually it was a city, lit up for the evening. Sometimes just an asphalt parking lot and another wing of the hotel across from it.

Someone coming here and looking out the window would see the expanse of the grounds and the mountains beyond that. It wouldn't be home, but it would feel like it.

Home. Garret felt like he hadn't had a home since he left Rockyview. He still didn't really have one. His apartment was adequate, sparsely furnished and utilitarian. This inn felt more like a home than his apartment did. He certainly spent more time here. Last night he was here until ten o'clock, weeding and trimming. He had come back to his apartment exhausted but feeling better than he had in years.

Garret let the emotions settle in his soul as above him the wind sighed through the trees, accompanied by the gurgling of Hidden Creek.

Peace and quiet. It had been years since he felt either, he thought, letting the tranquility wash over him. Working here was like being on a retreat. This place had so much potential.

Potential that would take years and a huge cash injection to realize.

As he entered the inn he saw Sheila checking in a young couple. They were laughing with her, looking forward to their holiday. They came to this inn trusting the staff to take care of them. Sheila pointed him out as the owner. They turned and smiled at him. "Lovely place you have here," they said as they walked past going up the large staircase to their room.

He glanced around the lobby again, trying to see it through their eyes. Through Larissa's eyes.

It was a lovely place, if you could look past the repairs that needed to be done. And once that work was done, it would look even more welcoming. Friendly.

Homey.

He let the thought settle, a part of his mind shifting to the woman sitting in the office. At one time he and Larissa had talked about where they would live. She had always said she wanted to live here. She said it was the best place in the world.

Now he was here after all, a part of the place and a part of the history.

Why not keep it? Why not be involved in something with roots? Why not be involved in something with Larissa?

He let the errant thought rest, trying to imagine what that would look like. At one time it would have been all he wanted.

The door to the office was still open and he could hear Larissa talking. He moved into the doorway, but Larissa no longer sat at the table. Instead she stood by the window with her back to him, holding the telephone.

"I'm not sure what to do, Dad," she was saying. "We put a huge dent in the operating loan on the kitchen renovations, which I wasn't crazy about...I know. I didn't agree with that either." She eased out a sigh. "No...I didn't bring it up." A long pause followed this. Obviously her father had a lot to say. "Of course I'll let you know what Garret wants to do. Hope the rest of the trip goes well. Thanks for the advice." Then she hung up.

She held the phone in one hand, resting her fisted hand under her chin as she looked out the window. From this angle Garret caught the troubled look on her face and while one part of him wondered what she was thinking, the other part of him felt a jolt of annoyance that she had wasted so little time contacting her father. Couldn't she make her own decisions? Was she still Daddy's girl as Emily had intimated?

He waited a moment, cleared his throat then stepped into the room.

She whirled around, puzzlement twisting her features. "I thought Pete wanted to see the grounds," she stammered, a flush creeping up her neck. "I thought you wouldn't be back for a while."

Obviously. Hence the call to Daddy to see what she should do. He wanted to be angry but a growing part of him felt sorry that she didn't think she could make her own decisions.

But for now they had business to discuss and one thing was certain—he knew he didn't want to do that sitting so close to her.

Letting his foolish thoughts take him places he could never go.

EIGHT

He looked angry, Larissa thought as Garret plucked a pad of paper from the desk. Had Pete said something to make him look so upset?

"Take your cell phone and some paper along," he said, his voice brisk and businesslike, his dark eyebrows pulled together in a frown. "We need to see who can do what for us in two weeks." Garret rolled up his sleeves, ready for work. "I'll meet you in the first room on the second floor," he said, then abruptly left.

Larissa picked up her phone, puzzled at the sudden shift in Garret's attitude. While Pete was here it felt as if she and Garret were moving to a better place in their relationship.

Well, as good a place as could be expected for a couple of exes who had parted on bad terms. But still.

Once in a while she had caught him looking at her and his smile had a warmth to it that hadn't been there before. She sensed something had changed between them and while she wasn't sure what it was, she didn't mind the shift in the constant tension humming between them.

She hurried up the stairs and found him standing in the middle of the first room, holding a tape measure, frowning at the room. "So we need to make a plan," he said. "We'll need quick and cheap."

Larissa pulled her pen from behind her ear and blew out a sigh. "Do you really think we can fix up the rooms in two weeks?"

"Not the way you'd like to, but we could probably do some superficial stuff. Some paint. Maybe some new bed coverings."

"Superficial seems like a waste of time and money," Larissa said. "Some of the walls need to be re-drywalled. The carpets need replacing. I really hoped we could redo the windows and install new doors. The bathrooms could use new fixtures."

Garret held his hand up at her list. "Unfortunately superficial is all we can afford right now. We don't have time to do everything you want in time for Pete's conference."

"So forget about Pete," Larissa snapped. "Do the work right and we can look for other business once we're done." She caught his frown and sensing his resistance, toned her anger down, trying to sound reasonable and professional. "We both want the same thing. We both want the inn to turn a profit and Pete just pointed out exactly what I'd been saying all along."

"If we don't get Pete, we might not get other business. I can't afford to put my own money into this business to buoy it up until things turn around," he retorted. "I'm not as well off as your father."

His words held a lash of anger that was unexpected and surprisingly hurtful.

Her mind ticked back to another time Garret had shown his anger with her over her father. They had fought about telling her parents about their relationship. He wanted things out in the open, but she was still afraid of what would happen when her father found out that she was dating Garret. Her father had never made any secret about his plans for her. He wanted her to go to university. Make a success of herself. He didn't want her to get married for a while. And she knew he certainly wouldn't want her to get married to someone who was working for him as a laborer.

As she held his narrowed gaze, she felt a surprising touch of regret at the shift in emotions. For just a few moments, when they were talking to Pete, she felt an accord between them. Now, it was swept away by the waves of frustration and anger washing over them both.

"Maybe I should talk to my father about the renos," she returned, refusing to be intimidated by Garret's increasing anger. "See what he thinks we should do."

"You don't have to go running to your father with every problem. Like I said, you have some control in this situation too. You have the power to make decisions."

She just stared at him, ice flowing through her veins in reaction to what he said.

"Running to my father?" she asked in a deliberate voice as her own anger grew. "What do you mean by that?"

Garret held her gaze, seemingly unintimidated by her fury. "I heard you talking to your dad after Pete left. I heard what you said."

"Last time I checked, he's a partner in the inn as well."

"Of course he is, but last time I checked you have some control and the power to make decisions as well. For now I think we need to take small steps. Maybe in time we can change the windows and do all the things you want, but for now we need to do things inexpensive and simple. And you can make that decision as easily as your father."

On one level Larissa heard what he was saying and felt assured by his confidence in her, but his comment still rankled and harkened back to some of the many discussions they'd had about her relationship with her father. "Now you resent my father's involvement, but when he stepped in years ago and offered you money to leave town, you were happy enough to take it."

As soon as the words left her mouth, Larissa wished she could recall them, but it was too late.

Garret only stared as the words fell between them, heavy as stones.

Yet as the silence between them grew and filled the room, she felt as if she had let go of a weight dragging her down for too many years. Finally, the whole reason for his leaving and her subsequent disillusionment was now out in the open.

"What do you mean by that?"

Larissa drew back at the controlled fury in his voice, but she held her ground and his gaze. She was seeing this through to the end. "You know exactly what I'm talking about."

Garret shook his head. "No. I do not."

Larissa wavered in the face of his decisiveness, but she also knew what her father showed her and forged ahead. "Are you telling me you didn't take the money my father gave you?" Her father had shown her the canceled check with Garret's scrawling signature on the back. "I know my father offered you money to leave. To leave me." She hated the way her voice broke. Why, after all these years, could that still bother her? "You took the check, you cashed it and then you left. Don't tell me that didn't happen."

The silence stretching between them was fraught with tension, hurt and sorrow.

"Then I have nothing to say to you. Because it didn't happen."

"So you didn't meet with my father at Mug Shots?" Larissa felt a quiver of uncertainty. Garret seemed so sure of himself.

"He met with me. Bit of a difference," Garret said, planting his hands on his hips. "Remember how we went to your parents' place to tell them about our relationship?"

"I remember you were uptight," Larissa said her mind casting back to that evening. The two of them sitting side by side on the leather settee in front of the fireplace, holding hands while they faced down her father. Garret had told her father that he cared for Larissa and that he wanted to let them know they were dating. Jack had said nothing at first. Then he nodded and looked directly at Garret. All he said was that he understood the situation and appreciated being told. As if he had been approached with some business decision.

"That was the first time I was ever in your parents' house. Of course I was uptight, but I was more uptight when he called me two days later and wanted me to meet him at Mug Shots."

"Was that when he gave you the check?" She didn't want to ask, but the words were drawn from her.

Garret frowned, as if thinking then his mouth curved in a cynical smile. "That's when he gave me *a* check."

His words were like ice to her heart. To hear him admit that extinguished the final, thin ray of hope.

"And you took it and cashed it."

"Of course I did. That check was for my wages and holiday pay. A thousand dollars. Your father essentially fired me and told me not to come back to the mill again."

Larissa blinked, trying to assimilate this information, but her mind caught on one detail. "But the check he made out to you was for ten thousand dollars, not a thousand."

"I wish," Garret snorted. "I wasn't that valuable an employee."

Larissa couldn't wrap her head around this information. "He showed it to me. I saw the figure. Ten thousand dollars. A one a zero, a comma and then three more zeros, a period and two more. Ten thousand."

She remembered how the amount had felt like an insult. Was that all she was worth to her father and to her old boyfriend. Ten thousand dollars?

"I guess I would know how much money I put in my bank account," Garret said. "And it was only a thousand."

Larissa frowned, unable to pull this all together. She would have to talk to her father about it. And what? Ask him how much the check really was for? He showed it to her. She saw the figure.

"You don't believe me," he said.

She shook her head in confusion rather than to negate what he had said. "I'm not sure what to think." Then she looked up at him, her confidence returning as the old emotions washed over her. "I just know you left. Does it matter how much money you had in your pocket?"

"It matters that you thought your father paid me to leave you alone."

"You still left," she insisted.

He tapped his fingers on his arm, his eyes flashing. "And you wouldn't talk to me after I did. I came to the house and you closed the door in my face."

They were going around in circles. Part of her wanted to forget the whole conversation and leave it buried in the past. Move on. But as she held his gaze older emotions swirled around them like a gathering storm and she knew they couldn't walk away from this. If they were going to work together in any kind of harmony, they had to put this out of the way.

"I didn't talk to you because I thought my father paid you to leave."

Garret slowly lowered his arms, heaving out a sigh. "Would you have talked to me if he hadn't shown you the check?"

She tried reaching back to what she had felt before she thought Garret had betrayed her. Then she nodded. "I cared for you. A lot," she said. "You meant more to me than anyone I've ever met." Too late she realized how that sounded. As if he'd been the only person in her life that had mattered to her.

Well, it's true, isn't it?

She stifled that errant question. Didn't matter. That was over. "So why did you leave?" She continued. "Why didn't you stay and fight for me? You could have worked somewhere else. We could still have been together."

Garret eased out a long, slow sigh, running his hand through his hair.

"When your father met with me at Mug Shots, he not only fired me, he told me exactly what he thought of our relationship. Nothing. He told me I wasn't good enough for you. Trouble was, he didn't have to tell me that. I knew that myself. Especially after I sat in the 'drawing room' of your parents' home." He made quotation marks with his fingers around the words "drawing room," his voice taking on a sardonic note.

"What do you mean by that?"

Garret folded his arms over his chest, his legs spread as if bracing himself, the light from the window behind him throwing his face into shadow. "I grew up in a small house on a ranch out in the boonies. I was working as a lumber piler, driving an old beat-up truck my grandfather and I would be fixing at least once a week because there was always something wrong with it. I was never ashamed of who I was or where I came from until I stepped inside your parents' house. I never fully realized how much you had grown up with until I saw that place."

"It's just a house," Larissa protested.

Garret shook his head. "It's a showpiece. Sitting in your parents' drawing room with its huge stone fireplace, leather furniture that probably cost what I made in a year, knowing there was still a family room, living room and library in the house, let alone the bedrooms and bathrooms. It reminded me of how far apart you and I really were."

"That didn't matter to me. I told you that."

Garret released a cynical laugh. "It mattered to me. I was a naive and stupid young man, thinking I could take you from that and expect that you would be happy living out on the ranch, and getting by on what I made working at the mill." Garret took a step closer. "I left because I knew I had to make some changes in my life. When your father gave me my severance pay, he told me I wasn't good enough for you and that I wouldn't be able to provide for you in the way you were used to. After I saw your house, I knew he was right."

"Why didn't you ask me what I wanted?" she asked.

"You told me what you wanted. You wanted to stay in Rockyview and you wanted me to work for your father. I thought you wanted me to become like your dad. Take care of you like your dad did."

His words nudged open a door to her past and she knew that, to some degree, he was right. She had hoped he would stay here and slowly become a part of the company and work his way up the business.

"What made it harder to stay—" Garret continued, "—was the fact that your dad told me if I didn't quit my job and leave town, he would fire me and make it difficult for anyone else to hire me. I knew I couldn't take care of you after he said that. So I didn't have much choice but to leave. Try to make something of myself somewhere else. I had always planned to return and had come to your house to tell you, but when you chose not to talk to me, I knew there was no reason to come back to Rockyview."

Larissa frowned, trying to assimilate what she knew about her father with what Garret was telling her. Had her father really threatened Garret?

Doubts and second thoughts fought each other in her mind. Her old feelings for Garret and the relationship they had rose to the surface, adding more fuel to the fire burning in her soul.

"Would you have come back if I had talked to you?" she finally asked.

As soon as the words left her lips she regretted the needy tone that slipped into her voice. She wasn't that girl anymore. She was independent. She'd dealt with huge things after Garret left. The illness and subsequent death of her mother. She'd kept the inn going in spite of her father's unwillingness to make any changes. She'd shown herself she didn't need anyone to complete her.

Then, to her surprise, Garret took one more step, closing the distance between them. He reached out and touched her cheek, his finger surprisingly rough against her skin.

"Once I felt like I could have taken care of you the way you were used to, yes. Yes, I would have come back."

His touch sent a tingle down her spine as his words cocooned her heart. Then, before she could stop herself, her hand came up and she wrapped her fingers around his, his skin warm and rough. They stood this way for a moment, past melding into present. Old fears and hurts being displaced by current feelings.

"Did you think about me while you were gone?" Her words slipped out, fueled by the lonely months that she had endured after he left. Moments fraught with anger and sorrow and the idea that she had meant so little to him.

He said nothing for a few long, silent seconds. Then he drew in a slow breath. "I never forgot you, Larissa. I thought of you all the time."

Garret's fingers tightened for a moment, but then he lowered his gaze and stepped away.

A flush warmed her cheeks and her heart did a slow flip in

her chest as his words seeped into her soul. Had he really thought of her all the time?

Get a grip, she reminded herself glancing around the room again, focusing herself on the job at hand. That was in the past.

Even as she tried to focus on what needed to be done, she knew she wouldn't forget his words.

"So, what should we start with in this room?" she asked, forcing herself to get on task.

Garret was silent a moment as if acknowledging the move to a safer topic, then walked around the room looking at it with a critical eye. "I really think if we do some superficial stuff for now—painting and new covers for the beds, maybe some cheap prints for the walls—we can go a long way with low financial output." He stopped at the window, his features in profile to her. Then she caught a hint of a smile as he rested his fingertips on the window ledge. "I think if we get rid of the curtains, the view can make up for a lot."

Larissa thought of the long hours he had put into maintenance the past week. "A view that, I must say, is improving every day," she added.

He nodded, one corner of his mouth tipping up in a smile. "It's been fun seeing the improvement." He flexed his arms and gave her a quick grin. "Though my arms and legs have been complaining."

The tone in his voice and the gentle lift of his lips as he looked out the window was almost as heartening as what had just happened between them. Was he learning to love the inn as she had come to? If so, that meant she had hope for the future.

Hope for the future of the inn, that is, she reminded herself.

GARRET HUNG up the phone and leaned back in his chair, linking his hands behind his head as he heaved out a frustrated sigh.

"Doesn't sound like you had any more luck than I did," he said, glancing across the table at Larissa.

She set her cell phone down, scratched another name on the pad of paper in front of her and shook her head. "Not quite a shutout, but close."

For the past hour they'd been trying to find someone, anyone who could do the painting job on such short notice. And even worse, Garret had a hard time concentrating on the conversations he was having with Larissa right across the table from him. He couldn't dismiss the moment of connection he'd felt upstairs, that feeling that things were right when he was with her.

Yet the entire time they worked upstairs, measuring and taking notes then coming down here and making phone calls, the idea that she thought her father had paid him ten thousand dollars was like an itch he couldn't scratch. How could she have thought that? What had Jack done to make her believe that?

He wished Jack were here so he could confront him and even as the thought was formulated in his mind, he pushed it back. And what purpose would that serve? He wasn't here to dig up past dealings with Jack Weir. He was here to establish himself in this town. To make a name for himself. Right now that meant trying to find a way to get the inn up to snuff in time for Pete's inspection trip.

"What do you have?" he asked, leaning forward.

Larissa tapped her pen against her mouth as she looked down at the paper. "The closest I came to success was with Benny Alpern," she murmured. "He said he had only enough time to do the prep work on all the rooms and the first coat on fifteen of them, so that's a start."

"How long would that take him?"

"About five days and he can come tomorrow."

Garret pulled at his lower lip, thinking. "Doesn't seem to be much point getting him to come period if he can't finish the job." Things weren't looking so positive and the job seemed daunting.

Larissa's only reply was to tap her pen harder, twisting her hair around her finger with her other hand. Just like she always did. He smiled at the sight, remembering how he used to tease her that if she didn't quit that habit, she'd end up bald.

"I still don't think we'll need all thirty rooms like Pete thinks," Larissa said. "Lots of people who come to these things double up to save money."

He pulled his focus back to the job at hand, surprised at the even tone of her voice.

The moment they had shared upstairs still clung to his soul and echoed in his mind.

He swept the tangling thoughts aside. He had no head-space to deal with that now.

"Doesn't matter what we think we need," he said, hunching over the papers with their endless rows of figures and numbers. "We need to get two coats of paint on those walls and that's just the beginning."

His head was growing tired, trying to work his way around this problem. It seemed insurmountable. "All that work and no one who can do it. It's hardly worth starting."

"Don't be such a Debbie Downer," Larissa mumbled, chewing on the end of her pen. "There's got to be a way to solve this."

"Debbie Downer?"

"Television character. Always looking on the dark side of life. You've never heard of her?"

"I never watch television."

"Not even those long, lonely nights in hotel rooms?"

He shook his head, the memory of those long, lonely nights in hotels still too recent. Sure, he lived in an apartment now, but coming here every day filled the space in his life that had been emptied when he moved away from his grandparents' ranch and Rockyview.

"I was always too busy to spend time watching television," he said.

"Busy doing what?"

"Working. Writing up reports, crunching numbers and scenarios, emailing, doing proposals, conference calls, chasing down paper trails. Sitting through endless meetings."

"No dates? No evenings out on the town?" She was smiling at him, but he sensed a puzzling undertone. As if she vaguely hinted at something else. "No girlfriend to keep you company?"

"A few. Here and there. I had a girlfriend for a few months, but it didn't take." Why did he think she needed to know that? And why did she seem to want to know?

He thought back to that little moment they shared in the room upstairs. The connection he couldn't shrug off.

"Really?" Larissa twirled her hair a bit harder. "That's too bad."

"Seems like you've been in the same situation," he said, leaning back in his chair, crossing his arms. If she could hint, so could he.

She lifted her shoulder in a vague gesture. "I've had a couple of...friends."

"I gather Pete was one of those...friends." That comment came out sharper than he intended and the puzzlement on her face showed him she had picked up on it.

"We dated for a while," she said, waving her pen in a dismissive gesture. "But as you can tell, whatever we had didn't make any difference in his booking the inn."

"Friends is friends and business is business," Garret said feeling a sudden burst of surprising jealousy. Did she still think about him? She didn't seem too bothered by it. In fact, Pete seemed to be doing more of the chasing than she did.

Suddenly she sat up and clapped her hands. "Friends is friends indeed. If its workers we need, I could call in a few favors," she said leaning forward, her hands clasped picking up some energy. "Get some of my friends to help. We could have a painting party."

Garret frowned. "Could they do a good job, though? We can't have paint all over the place."

"Now, Debbie," Larissa said wagging her finger at him.

Garret laughed again, stifling his next objection.

"We'd have to supervise, of course," Larissa continued, "Which would mean extra work for us, but I'm sure we could get the work done properly. Especially if we've got Benny doing the prep work and the first coat. That's the fussy work. The rest is just production."

"Could we get it done on time?"

"I'm positive we can," she said, picking up her cell phone, her eyes sparkling with anticipation.

"That's just the painting. What about the furnishings?"

"If I get enough people painting, Alanna and I can head up to Highlands and get some fun and funky bedding at that store that started up— My House and Yours. I know they've got some really good deals going on now. We could do every room a bit different. Like a cross between a B&B and an inn. What do you think?"

"Do you really think we can get enough people together? And how would we pay them?"

She frowned. "Pay them?"

"We certainly can't expect people to come here and help us out for nothing?"

"You don't think your family would want to help you out?"

He returned her frown, not sure what to think. "This is a business. Why would they want to help me?"

Larissa sat back, her one arm folded across her midsection, her fisted hand resting under her chin as she seemed to be studying him. "Friends may be friends, but I'm sure family falls under another category. Besides that's what family does for each other. That's what a community does for each other. When Kerry needed painting done at Mug Shots, a bunch of us all pitched in and helped. Mia, Alanna, myself. When Mia Verbeek moved out of her house we all helped out. It's what you do when you live in a community."

Garret held her gaze, aware that while she was looking at him, she nodded, her grin growing. "Watch me make some Rockyview magic," she said and started punching in numbers on her cell phone.

Garret couldn't help pick up on her energy, her enthusiasm. As she started scribbling a list of potential candidates and talking to her friend Alanna, he found himself unable to look away. Unable to not be drawn into her smile, the sparkle in her eyes, the enthusiasm in her voice.

He tried to remind himself that she was his business partner and not his old girlfriend.

But he found the more time he spent with her, the harder that got to be.

NINE

"So for today I've got Hailey in the yellow room and Sabine and Tanner doing one of the blue rooms. Alanna and I will be doing the green room and Kerry and Evangeline are in the gray room. Tricia said she might come and so did Summer."

Garret looked over Larissa's chart, nodding as she showed him her plan, the smell of fresh paint filling his nostrils. "Looks like we'll get done by today if all goes well," he said. The panic that had gripped him since he made his rash promise to Pete was slowly easing with each day of progress. "I still can't believe you got all this done so quickly and with minimal interference to our other guests."

Larissa nodded, her head down, but to Garret's surprise he saw a flush working its way up her neck. Was she embarrassed by his praise?

"It took a bit of organizing, but your family has been a great help." She looked up at him then and her smile dove into his soul. "And thanks for helping as well."

Her hair was held back by a paint-speckled bandanna and

smudges of paint decorated her cheek and the oversize shirt she wore over her clothes. And still, she looked beautiful.

"Hey, I've got a vested interest in turning this place around. It's been kind of exciting to see the changes the past few days." He held her gaze, the warmth of her smile creating an answering warmth deep in his soul. "Sort of like seeing this place rising up and being restored to its former glory."

Her smile grew, her expression softened. "I've always gotten the impression that the only reason you wanted to do anything to this inn was to make it profitable for profit's sake."

"It's a business, of course that's a priority, but at the same time I have to think of what you said about this being a place of refuge for travelers..." His voice trailed off as he looked past her to a room that had already been painted, trying to imagine what it would like when it was all completed. He turned back to her, feeling a bit embarrassed at his little outburst. "Anyhow, it's looking good."

"That means a lot to me," she said.

Their gazes held and once again old emotions laced with newer ones arced between them. He let his gaze rest on her face so familiar, and yet so different.

Older. More mature. More confident.

More beautiful, if that was possible.

He had to fight the urge to reach out and tuck a stray strand of hair back under the bandanna.

He felt his hand rising up.

"Just the people I need to talk to."

Garret groaned as Mrs. Rochester's voice broke into the moment.

He turned to face the housekeeper, dredging up a smile. "What can we do for you?"

"I can't work around this," she said, waving her hand at the plastic-covered hallway. "I can't possibly do what needs to be done each evening up here. It's a disaster."

"Why don't we talk about this downstairs?" Larissa said, taking Mrs. Rochester's arm and easing her away from Garret. "I'm sure we can come to an agreement."

But before she left Larissa shot Garret a warm smile that did nothing for his equilibrium. "I just have to take care of this," she said.

"Yes. Sure. Okay." He took a step back, then spun around and strode down the hallway, entering the room he had been assigned to work on with his cousin.

"What's wrong with you?" Hailey asked as he picked up the paint roller. "You look like someone just kicked your dog."

"I don't have a dog," Garret retorted, hoping Hailey wouldn't connect his confused emotions with his meeting with Larissa out in the hallway.

"I guess we're not talking about your little chat with Larissa, though I can't figure out what she said that would have put that grumpy look on your face." Hailey dipped her brush in the paint and carefully coated the corner of the wall.

It wasn't what Larissa said that bothered him, Garret thought, rolling the butter-yellow paint over the whitish-gray undercoat. It was how she looked. How she sounded.

How, in spite of being liberally sprinkled with paint, he could still catch the scent of her perfume.

And that's enough.

"Larissa sure picked out some nice colors," Hailey was saying.

"Yeah. She did."

"Got a good eye," Hailey added with a knowing wink.

Garret rolled some more paint on the wall, ignoring his cousin's knowing smirk.

"I can't believe Larissa conned you into helping. I thought

you were supposed to be walking around, looking all managerial, cracking the whip and keeping us on task," Hailey teased.

"I've painted before," Garret said, dipping his roller in the tray. "This way I can keep the most unruly of our workers in line, though I really appreciate the help."

When Larissa first mentioned getting people to paint, Garret wondered who would be willing. But he underestimated both Larissa's ability to sweet-talk and the generosity of the community. And he had underestimated the connections of his own family. The last couple of days the inn was a beehive of activity and, surprisingly, laughter as friends and neighbors and family all pitched in.

"I'm helping because I have a stake in getting this place shipshape," Hailey said, getting off her chair and moving it so she could finish up around the window. "Though we have the church and hall booked as a backup, Shannon and I still dream of having our weddings here."

"I don't know what shape the grounds will be in by then."

"You've done a ton of work already," Hailey said.

"And there's about five ton that needs to be done yet." Garret thought of the overgrown tangle of shrubs and trees he hadn't had a chance to work on. "And that crazy grass keeps growing."

"We could all help with that too," Hailey said, shooting a glance over her shoulder. "I've pushed a mower a time or two in my life. Even ran the riding mower at the ranch."

"I hope your mowing skills have improved since then," Garret said, his smile growing as his mind slipped back in time. "I remember a run-in with Nana's lilac bush and a detour through the garden."

"You still blaming a faulty throttle on me?" Hailey said in mock horror, pressing a paint-stained hand against her chest. "Besides, the lilac bush needed some trimming and I believe there's still a dent in Naomi's cabin from when you hit it with the same mower with the same faulty throttle."

Garret laughed, surprised at the raft of memories filling his mind since spending time with his family. "Speaking of Naomi, I heard she's coming back in a couple of weeks."

Hailey's smile faded as she nodded. "Yeah. I'm surprised my dear sister stayed in Halifax as long as she did."

"A month after her fiancé died isn't that long."

"I just wished she would have come here. So we could have helped her through this time."

Garret felt a touch of sorrow for his cousin Naomi. "I'm surprised at her strength. I talked to her yesterday and she seemed so calm."

"That's our Naomi. Always the strong, quiet one." Hailey tapped her paintbrush against the container she held and released a melancholy laugh. "As opposed to me who can never keep her mouth shut. Or your brother, Tanner, who is having a little bit too much fun. You might want to go check on him when you're done here." Her smile returned along with a mischievous sparkle in her eye. "Or you could see what Larissa is up to."

Garret looked away as he rolled some more paint on the wall. The help was great but Hailey's constant innuendos concerning Larissa he could do without. "Larissa has Alanna working with her."

Thankfully Hailey said nothing more on that topic but as they worked they talked about the ranch, their nana, the community and Hailey even touched on Garret's church attendance.

He didn't mind. Since coming back he was surprised how easily he slipped into the lives of his cousins and how quickly he had found his own place here.

He let his mind drift a bit more, letting himself look to the future and wondering what shape it would take.

Whom he might be with.

"This is awesome. You guys have done a great job."

Larissa's voice behind him gave him a start and he spun around.

"Looks like you got more paint on yourself than the wall," Garret said.

Larissa looked down at her shirt laughing. "Alanna tried to have a paint fight. I held her off, but this was the result."

"A paint fight? At thirty-two dollars a gallon?"

"Alanna can be such a child," Larissa said. Then she held up her phone. "By the way, just got a call from My House and Yours in Highlands. They have a new shipment in of duvet covers. I'm going in and check them out."

"Now?" Garret glanced at his watch. It was already three p.m. in the afternoon and Highlands was an hour's drive away. "Cutting it a bit close, aren't you?"

"I don't have time to go tomorrow or the day after." She glanced at Hailey. "I'm guessing you're done here."

"You're guessing right," Hailey said stepping off the chair. "We'll come back tomorrow and do the other room."

Then Larissa held up her phone. "I should get going."

"Do you need me to come?" Garret asked.

"You don't need to."

Garret wasn't sure if she was giving him an out or being understanding, but he felt as if he should go along. He didn't want her making all the decisions about the inn.

It had nothing to do with spending time with her. This was strictly professional, he told himself.

On another level, however, he knew it was an excuse to spend some more time with her. To find out what was going on between them.

Because he knew something was.

"Most everyone is done here and Sheila said she would stay for a while longer," he said, glancing at his watch. "She can make sure we don't have any more disgruntled customers."

"Okay then, let's go," Larissa said, surprising him with her lack of resistance. Was she also sensing his growing awareness of her? Did she feel the same?

Garret sent his cousin a quick wave goodbye, ignoring Hailey's faint smirk.

This was business. Nothing more. That was the only reason he was going along.

So why did his heart quicken at the thought of spending some time with Larissa away from the inn? Away from the constant stream of people?

TEN

"I can't believe we got everything we needed," Larissa said, trundling one of the laden carts toward the exit of the store.

"And we did it without bloodshed," Garret joked, following Larissa with his own cart. "Though it's pretty hard to draw blood when your only weapons are sheets and pillowcases."

Larissa's pealing laugh warmed him. "You had your chance when we picked up pictures and frames for the rooms. Those things have sharp corners."

"The mood had passed by then," he said with a grin, pleased at what they had accomplished in such a short time.

Yet, he knew there was more to the feeling of goodwill that wrapped him as comfortingly as the duvets they had just purchased.

This time with Larissa, away from the inn, away from other people, allowed him to feel more relaxed around her. Gave him a chance to sort out his changing feelings and try to figure out what he should do about them.

Try to understand why she thought he would have taken

her father's money. The tentative conversation on the subject hadn't been enough. He felt that if they could resolve the money issue once and for all, their business relationship would go more smoothly. Because whether he liked it or not, Jack would return from his extended stay in Asia and he was as much a partner in this business as Garret was. Larissa held the balance of power and he would prefer that she was on his side, rather than Jack's.

Yet, even as he thought that, he knew there were deeper underlying reasons he wanted to remove the barriers the past had put between them. He wasn't ready to examine them too closely, but for now he wanted to nurture the ray of hope that sprung up in his chest when he touched her cheek and she gave him a genuine smile in return.

They stepped outside the store and Garret was surprised to see the sun hovering above the horizon. In the store, with its bright lights and lack of windows, time had stood still.

"I didn't know it was this late," Larissa said, glancing at her watch as she parked the cart by the car. "My goodness, seven o'clock already."

"Lunch was a long time ago," Garret grumbled as he opened the back door. As he took the packages from Larissa, the blinking lights of a restaurant caught his eye. "You as hungry as I am?" he asked, glancing back at Larissa.

"Actually, yes," she said.

"So why don't we grab a bite to eat at that restaurant over there?" he asked, indicating with his chin as he continued loading the parcels into the back of the car. "We can leave the car here and walk over."

"Sounds like a good idea." Larissa's quiet response was accompanied by a careful smile, which only served to ignite the flicker of hope glowing in his soul the past few days.

He knew he should be careful. He had come to Rockyview with a plan. Yet, as he and Larissa strode over the almost deserted parking lot to the restaurant, a sense of anticipation washed over him. Anticipation he sensed had been building between them ever since he admitted to her that he had never forgotten her.

When they got to the restaurant and he was settled into a booth across from Larissa, her hair shining in the lights of the restaurant, a gentle smile hovering on her lips, his anticipation grew and settled into the part of his soul that had been empty ever since he walked away from Rockyview and Larissa all those years ago.

The waitress handed him a menu, a tall black affair with a padded cover and the name of the restaurant printed in raised gold letters on the front. When they had stepped inside the restaurant and he saw the brick fireplace flanking the entrance and the waterfall behind the hostess desk, he had an inkling supper wasn't going to be cheap.

Larissa waited until their friendly waitress was out of earshot, then closed her menu and leaned forward with a concerned expression. "We don't have to eat here. Have you seen these prices?"

"I've seen worse," he said, unable to resist adding a wink.

"We could just go get a burger," she said lowering her voice.

Garret reached over, and opened her menu to the entrée section. "You know what? In all the time we were dating I never had a chance to take you anywhere but Mug Shots. Let me at least make up for that by treating you to a nice dinner here."

Larissa tilted her head, as if trying to see him from a new angle, her gaze holding his, a quizzical expression on her face.

"I've got paint spatters on my face."

"I probably do too," he said easing out a smile, surprised at the emotions wavering between them. "But I always wanted to do this for you. To let you know how special you were to me." The words slipped out before he could stop them.

"Was I special to you?"

He recognized the hesitantly spoken question for what it was. They were slipping into a new and different place, one still tinged with the past.

"Yes. You...were." He wanted to tell her that she still was but he wasn't sure that was a place they should go right away. Emotions were still unsteady between them, but at the same time, he felt his own feelings shifting.

She looked down at the menu, running her thumb along the edge of it. "When we were talking, a few days back, about...about my father and what happened in the past, you seemed to think I had certain expectations of you when we were dating."

"What do you mean?"

Larissa fingered a strand of hair away from her face and even in the dim light of the restaurant he saw the paint spatters she was so concerned about still decorating her forehead. He thought of the one he had smoothed off her face and how surprised he'd been at his own reaction to touching her.

"You made it sound as if I thought you should keep me in the manner to which I was accustomed."

He released a quiet sigh, trying to figure out where to go from here. "I did feel that way and like I said before, I felt pretty inadequate when I saw your house and how you had grown up. I didn't think I deserved to take care of you."

Larissa's smile grew melancholy. "Part of me understands that," she said quietly. Then she looked up at him, holding his gaze, her own surprisingly intent. "I guess I would have liked to have been given a chance to prove that idea wrong."

Garret heard the disappointment in her tone and let it

settle. For the first time since he walked away from Rockyview, he realized how unfair his assumptions about her had been. He reached over and covered her hand with his. "I'm sorry. I shouldn't have presumed money was so important to you. But I also want you to know that I didn't want to take the chance that it might have caused a problem for us later on."

Larissa twisted her hand so that her fingers twined with his and she tightened her grip. "Was that check really only for a thousand dollars?"

Garret stifled a note of impatience at the return to this touchy subject but at the same time grasped that this needed to be dealt with. The check was a stumbling block for her and had instigated a chain of events that had pushed them apart. Looking at the situation through her eyes he realized that she had equated the check with her own value.

"That day in Mug Shots, your father wrote out a check to me for a thousand dollars. That was all. He told me it was my severance pay." He squeezed back. "If he was trying to pay me to leave, and if I thought I could have taken care of you the way I wanted to, then no check could have been big enough."

Larissa's smile wavered a moment and as their eyes held it was as if everything around them, all the years between them fell away.

"I wish—"

Garret reached over and touched his finger to her lips, silencing her regrets.

"What's done is done," he said quietly, tracing the shape of her mouth and then letting his hand do what his heart wanted and cupped her chin. His fingers caressed her cheek and it was as if time wheeled backward and paused, waiting for what would happen next.

She reached up and covered his hand with hers, and old

connections and emotions were rekindled and brought into this moment.

"When I told you I never stopped thinking about you, I want you to know that I meant it," he said, his voice surprisingly husky with emotion. "I thought about you all the time I was away. I measured every woman I met by your standard."

Her smile softened and he caught a faint glistening in her eyes. "I shouldn't have let you go," she said quietly.

"So have you decided what you wanted?"

Their waitress's overly cheerful voice grated into the moment.

Garret stifled a sharp retort at the unwelcome interruption. The girl was just doing her job. She didn't know how she had broken the mood.

So he withdrew his hand, and dragged his attention back to the huge menu.

He made a random selection, not bothering to look at the price or even what it was. Larissa took a little more time, holding up the menu between her and Garret as if she needed the space to decide what to think.

She gave her order. The waitress smiled and took their menus, asked if they needed anything else, then finally left.

Garret waited until she was gone, then folded his hands on the table, and leaned forward feeling a sudden need to take charge. "We may as well get right to it," he said. "I think we've wasted enough of our time. I think we both know something's happening between us. I don't want to ignore it, and act as if nothing is going on. I can't do that."

"You really haven't changed," Larissa said with a gentle laugh.

"What do you mean?"

"You were always such a no-nonsense guy." Then Larissa

reached across the table, and pulled his hand toward hers, turning it over and tracing her finger over his palm. "I always liked that about you. In many ways you reminded me of my father."

Garret wanted to pull his hand back at the mention of Jack. The man who, it seemed had created so many problems between them by firing Garret and lying to Larissa.

He knew how Larissa adored her father and looked up to him. She sincerely thought she was giving him a compliment. So he let it slide.

Focus on the now, he reminded himself. Jack Weir doesn't have the power over you that he used to.

And right now it's all about you and Larissa.

"Your hands look like they've done lots of hard work," Larissa was saying as she traced a scar on his thumb. She turned his hand over and ran her finger across another one across the back. "Did the work you did when you left Rockyview put these there?"

Garret recognized this opportunity for what it was. A chance to catch up and fill in the intervening years. To connect their present with their past.

"I worked an oil field for the summer, just to get some money together. It was hard, rough work. Then in the fall I went to school and kept working as a roughneck over the summer to pay my way."

"What made you choose engineering?"

"I was good in math," he said with a shrug. "And a friend of mine told me it was a good job that made good money."

"That was important to you?" Her question held a tinge of old doubts. That stupid check again.

"Yes, but I want you to know why," Garret said quietly as he took her other hand in his, her gentle touch easing away the loneliness of all these past years. "When my mother found out she was pregnant with twins, my father said he couldn't afford to take care of three people and bailed on her. She never heard from him again, so when she was about eight months pregnant, she moved back to my nana and grandpa's ranch. After we were born, she got a job. She was determined to support herself. She worked her way up and ended up finally able to support us on her own. Then, when I was about eight, I came home from a friends and found my mother in the kitchen, crying, sitting at the table, holding a piece of paper. A letter telling her that she was fired. She begged me not to tell Nana and Papa or even Tanner. She was so ashamed." Garret stopped there. He couldn't tell her the letter was signed by her father.

Tanner had been gone with a friend on a week-long camping trip and Nana and Papa were gone for a couple of days, visiting. So it was just him and his mother. He had to watch her grow more and more despondent every day. As soon as Nana and Papa came back, she left. Never came back to the ranch. A year later she was dead.

Larissa's fingers continued to trace gentle circles around his hand but a troubled expression flitted across her face.

"Wasn't your mother working at the sawmill?" she asked, drawing her own conclusions.

"Yeah. She was."

Larisa caught one corner of her lip between her teeth, as if thinking. "Was it my father who fired her?"

Garret only nodded.

"When did she die?"

Garret sensed where she was going with this. "My mother died of cancer a year later. It had nothing to do with your dad firing her."

Larissa looked down, as if ashamed. "I'm sorry. I'm sorry

about your mother, and I'm sorry that my father had to do that to her."

"It's not your fault," Garret said tightening his grip on her hands. "You had nothing to do with your father's decisions." And as he spoke those words, he held them a moment, let them settle into his life.

On one level he had always known what happened to his mother had nothing to do with her father, but he had clung to the injustice of it all. That was one reason he decided to get a job working at the same mill his mother had been fired from. To show Jack Weir that he was capable. Worthy of working for him.

Tanner had never carried the same burden, but then Tanner hadn't been at home to watch his mother sink deeper and deeper into despair and then, finally, leave.

However the past few weeks he'd been involved in something that gave him a surprising amount of pleasure. And it had less to do with trying to find a way to best Jack Weir and more to do with building a business that was a part of a community.

A business that had a future that he could see himself sharing with Larissa.

"Maybe not, but I spent a lot of time defending him. Thinking that everything he did was right." Larissa tried to pull her hand back, but Garret wouldn't let her. "I feel like the last few weeks have made me look at my father differently. Something you said really underlined that for me. When you told me I had a choice. That I had some power in making decisions." She looked up at him then, her eyes shining with a light of conviction. "No one's ever told me that before. No one's ever given me control." Her voice held authority and confidence that he'd never heard before. "I know, to some degree you had been saying it before, but it's like it all came together since I started working with you. When we were in the store just now,

I almost called my father to ask him what he thought. Then I remembered what you said and realized I didn't need to. That if you and I agreed on this, we could go ahead. I didn't need his approval."

Garret wasn't sure what to say. He knew some of the things he had told her had been spoken out of anger and exasperation when it seemed to him that Larissa hadn't changed. That she was still determined to be her father's daughter and try to please him.

But the certainty in her voice underlined her words and removed another barrier between them. Smoothed out another rough patch.

"You are your own person," he told her. "You always were. I'm glad you're able to see yourself for who you really are."

Larissa's smile grew. "I'm glad you were able to help me get there."

He was about to say more when their waitress arrived with their food. They sat back, letting her lay steaming plates of food in front of them, refill their glasses of water, ask if they needed anything else and then, thankfully, leave.

Garret picked up his fork and poked at the mound of pasta on his plate, frowning. "What is this?"

"What you ordered." Larissa grinned. "You don't remember?"

Garret shrugged as he unfolded the thick cloth napkin and laid it on his lap. "Doesn't matter. My nana always told me I had to eat what was put in front of me so I guess I'll find out."

"Speaking of your grandmother, we never did finish talking about how you got to where you are now," Larissa said, unfolding her own napkin. "What made you finally decide to come back home?"

The wistfulness in her voice pierced him with guilt. He forestalled his answer by pushing a pasta noodle around his dish. "My nana had a heart attack. I wasn't here when it happened. No one was except my cousin Shannon. When I heard that, I knew I had to figure out a way to come back home but I was stuck in the middle of an important job in Dubai and there was no way I could get out of it. So I made a quick trip back when she was out of the hospital, then left again."

"You came back for Sabine and Tanner's wedding."

He nodded, finally stabbing the elusive noodle and looking up at her. "That was another quick back and forth trip. At that time I had another big job going."

"Which also made you good money."

Garret heard the faint censure in her voice.

"Yes. It did." He finally put his fork down sensing they had this to get out of the way as well. "You need to know that neither my mother nor my grandparents had much money. My mother was a single parent trying to raise us on minimum wage jobs. My grandfather's ranch did okay, but he had to struggle through some horrible cattle prices and some bad drought years. When my mother got the job at the mill we thought things were turning around. Then she got...lost that job. When I saw what my mother and my grandfather went through I promised myself that wouldn't happen to me. I was going to be in charge of my life and I figured the only way to do that was to have money. Then I met you and my plans changed."

"What do you mean?"

"You know what I mean," he said, smiling at the coy inflection in her voice.

She shrugged, her smile creating a dimple in one cheek. "I kind of do, but I want to create a timeline."

"When I met you I realized I wanted to settle down. I wanted to make a home and I wanted to support you properly."

Her smile faded at that. "And you thought you could until

you saw the inside of my house. A house, you may as well know, my mother inherited from her father along with the inn."

"Doesn't matter. It was still your home. How well-off you were never completely sunk in until I came inside it. Then I knew I was fooling myself to think money didn't matter. Especially when I saw what your father was able to do to me." In spite of her desire to establish a timeline, he wished they didn't have to talk about this. He didn't want to delve into the past. Yet he had a sense that if they could resolve the past, they stood a chance at having a future.

"So I became determined to show myself and anyone else that I was in charge of my own life," he continued. "That money was going to make the difference for me. When I invested in a small mining IPO that exploded, I made even better money. Which made me able to buy a share in the inn when I finally decided to come back. And here I am. Partners with you."

Larissa cut up a piece of veal and stabbed it with her fork. "Except it was really the sawmill you wanted, wasn't it?"

Garret nodded. "Yeah. It was. The reality was the mill makes more money."

"Which is important to you."

"*Was* important to me." As he spoke those words Garret realized he meant them. He didn't have to say them just to please her. "I love working at the inn more than I thought possible. I enjoy seeing people coming and going and especially now that we're making all these changes, I'm pretty excited to see the end result."

Larissa's smile grew at that.

"And I like being partners with you," he added. "I like working with you. Making plans with you."

"I'm not really a partner," she corrected.

"Yes, you are. You do know you hold the balance of power,"

he teased, taking a quick bite of his rapidly cooling food. "If your father and I disagree on something, you can determine which way the business should go."

"You said that before."

"Which is why I'm taking you out to dinner tonight. To bribe you to take my side." He spoke the words lightly, trying to inject a more humorous tone, but deep down a part of him wondered what Larissa would do if he and her father couldn't agree.

"You didn't need to do that." She spoke the words quietly but with assurance. "For the first time since I took over the inn I feel like I'm working with someone who has direction and a plan for the inn. The inn means so much to me and I really want to see it return to the days when it was making money. I know it can. It's been hard to...well, to portray that to my father and get him on board with my ideas. I'm so glad you are as enthusiastic about the inn as I am."

Her sincerity and muted passion resurrected a sense of guilt. His initial purpose for the success of the inn had been different than hers.

As he held her sincere gaze he recognized that over the past couple of weeks his priorities had shifted. Yes, he still wanted the inn to succeed, but if he really delved into his motivation for that he knew he would find different reasons.

The main one being the woman sitting across the table from him. When he started working with her he had been determined to protect himself by keeping her at arm's length.

However, in the past few weeks, that had not only been more difficult, it had begun to matter less. Especially once he found out about the misinformation her father had fed her. A lie that had kept her away from him.

He suppressed a burst of anger at what Jack had done to them. The years they had wasted.

He couldn't indulge in that now. For now he was with Larissa and for the first time in years, he felt a measure of peace and belonging. He dared allow himself to think about a future that extended beyond the next paycheck. The next job.

And in the muted light of the restaurant as he looked into Larissa's eyes, he wondered if she might be part of that future.

"I want the inn to succeed," he said quietly, pushing his unfinished food aside. He wasn't hungry after all. "And I'm sure with enough work and dedication, it will."

Larissa's smile reinforced his opinion.

"So what do you think we need to do yet before Pete comes?" she asked, bringing the conversation back to business.

"Get the rooms ready. I'm excited to see everything come together, the spreads, the pillows with the colors we've painted the rooms."

"I understand you got Scrap Happy to move their mini-scrapbooking and card-making conference from The Pines here."

"They're still a tentative. I think Renee is waiting to see if Pete books with us before she makes her decision."

Garret hardly dared to think Pete might not book. Though he and Larissa had a fun and successful shopping trip, the reality was they were rapidly reaching the end of the operating loan. If Pete said no—

He stopped that thought. Didn't dare even let it enter the edges of his mind.

"He'll do it," Larissa said quietly. "I know he will." She squeezed his hand and he returned her smile. "I'm praying he will."

"Then the poor guy doesn't have much of a chance does he?" Garret returned.

"Hopefully not," Larissa said.

Their conversation moved to the other changes they

wanted to make. They talked about the grounds. About the roof. Boring, mundane stuff at one time, but for the first time in his life, Garret felt as if he was a part of something important. Not a business, but a calling.

And working with Larissa was making that even more important to him.

ELEVEN

Larissa laid her head back on the seat of Garret's car. The hum of the tires on the road and the heat inside the car created a lethargy she had a hard time shaking off. It was too dark to see the details of the mountains but there was enough light in the sky yet to see their silhouette.

Though she had lived her entire life in the shadow of the mountains, she never tired of seeing them in the changing light and in the changing seasons.

She rolled her head to look at Garret, his face in profile as he watched the road ahead. She recognized the man she had been in love with in the set of his jaw and the slope of his forehead. His thick hair seemed as untamed as ever.

Her heart did a slow flip as he turned his head.

"What are you thinking?" he asked, his voice gentle.

She wasn't ready to reveal her true thoughts, so she reverted to the surface emotions. "I'm glad we spent some time together away from the inn and away from everyone else."

Garret's slow smile gave her heart another flip and when he

reached over and stroked her cheek, her heart went into overdrive.

"I'm glad too," he said quietly, then reached over and, just like he used to, twined his fingers through hers and let their joined hands rest on his knee.

A bridge between past and present, Larissa thought.

Things had changed between them. The tension between them had shifted and been replaced by a sense of waiting for something else to happen.

Garret gazed up through the windshield at the mountains ahead.

"What are you looking for?" Larissa asked.

"The Shadow Woman."

"But you can only see her when the sun shines on the mountain at a certain time of the day. It's too dark now."

"It's an old habit. Whenever my brother and I would come to town with Nana and Papa, Tanner and I had a contest to see who would see her first."

"Who won?"

"Whoever managed to be sitting in the front of the truck." Garret shot her a quick grin. "That was usually me."

"My mother said there was a story behind the shadow."

"I'm not exactly sure. Me and my cousins always thought it was Nukinu, our Sarcee great-great-grandmother on my grandfather's side of the family, waiting for her lost love to return, but my nana always said Nukinu wasn't the kind of person to wait around."

"My mom has talked about Nukinu and a legend of some gold nuggets. What was that story about?"

"Apparently our great-great-grandmother was a native woman whose father had traded with a Kootenai for gold nuggets. He gave them to Nukinu, telling her to never tell anybody else about them. He had seen what gold fever did to their people, and to the white people who came seeking it. And then one day, August Bond, my great-great-grandfather came to the valley. He was looking for gold but fell in love with Nukinu. However, when she showed him the gold nuggets her father had given her, the gold fever came back. So he left her and went looking. Then one day he was trudging through the wet bush, hungry, following yet another creek up the mountain and looked down into the valley. He realized how stupid it was to go looking for something that was elusive and wouldn't satisfy. So he packed up his shovel and came back down the mountain looking for Nukinu. He asked her forgiveness and then he asked her to marry him." Garret smiled at the story.

"What happened to the gold nuggets?"

"They were put into a bracelet which was passed down to the family, until my grandfather gave the bracelet to my nana. After her heart attack, she had the bracelet made up into five necklaces. When each of us kids came back, she gave us each a necklace and a Bible. The necklace was to show us where we had come from, and the Bible was to show us where we are going." Garret released a short laugh. "I seemed to always know where I came from. I just didn't always know where I was going."

"What do you mean?" Larissa asked. She had an idea but at the same time she wanted to hear his take on what had kept him going all these years.

Garret was quiet a moment, his fingers tightening around hers, his eyes watching the road as it wound along the edge of the mountain.

"I often thought I was like August Bond. I never told you this before, but I think you need to know. I was always determined to work for your father's mill. I was still an angry young man who wanted to find a way to get back at Jack for what I perceived was an injustice when he fired my mother."

He stopped there, glancing at her, then away.

"And then," she prompted the tiniest chill entering her heart.

"Then I met you and I thought I had found the perfect way to get even."

The chill grew and she tried to pull her hand away, but Garret wouldn't let her.

"But I made a huge mistake," he said, holding tightly to her hand. "I fell for you. My plans blew away like sawdust in the wind." He looked her way. "It all changed when I met you. My focus, my plans. All the things I wanted to do. They all changed the first time I saw you standing just past the edger."

Larissa clearly remembered the jolt of attraction she felt when she saw him. The sudden feeling that everything in her world had shifted. "I know what you mean," she said quietly.

"After...I left Rockyview, I reverted back to that guy. The one who would show them. I wasn't coming back until I could show everyone what a success I'd made of myself." He shot another look her way. "But while I was gone I never felt complete. I had wandered away from all the things my grandparents had instilled in me. I wandered away from my faith and lost my way."

"And now?"

Garret drew in a long, slow breath. "I keep saying the reason I came back to Rockyview was my grandmother. But I think, deep down inside, the real reason I came back was you."

The hum of the tires and the faint tick of his keys against the steering column were the only noises in the silence following his declaration.

His words seeped into her soul, filling places bereft from his leaving. She wanted to hold on to each word, each nuance in his voice, and store them away to analyze later.

"I'm glad you're back," she said quietly.

Garret's expression grew serious and then to her surprise, he slowed the car down, its headlights sweeping across the pavement as he steered into one of the many lookout points along this highway.

"Is something wrong?" she asked sitting up as he parked the car and then, turned it off.

He kept his eyes ahead, and then he got out of the car. Curious about what was going on, she followed him.

He leaned against the hood of the car, the air picking up a coolness from the water rushing below them.

In the half-light she caught the glint of Hidden Creek tumbling over the rocks, an endless flow of water that would pass through the property of the inn before flowing into Rockyview, close to the center of town.

"You know, it's kind of interesting that both my brother and I now own property along this creek, but in different places," Garret said, his hands resting on the hood of the car behind him. "I never thought that would happen."

Larissa said nothing, letting him determine where this conversation was going. She wasn't sure what was happening, but for now she was willing to see where it went.

Then Garret turned to her and cupped her face in his hand, as if it was the most natural thing in the world to do. "I never thought that this would happen either," he added, his fingers cool on her heated cheeks.

It felt right. It felt good.

Larissa shut off her second thoughts. Shut off her doubts and, turning, pressed her lips against Garret's hand.

"Where are we going?" Garret's question was a quiet whisper as he slipped his other hand around her waist, pulling her close.

"If you don't know, I can't tell you," Larissa joked, trying to find an equilibrium in the emotions that had been in flux all evening.

"I feel as if we're coming full circle," Garret said, his hand slipping down her face, cradling her neck.

"Is that a good thing?"

Garret's eyes, glinting in the growing dusk, seemed to pierce hers. "I don't know."

His answer wasn't encouraging and yet, as she looked into his eyes as she felt his hands around her waist, she felt a sense of rightness so strong, so real, she couldn't stop her own hands from slipping up his chest and clasping his neck.

It was like a dance they both knew the steps to. A rhythm she could never find with anyone else.

And when he bent his head to kiss her and she raised her lips to his, it was as if she was coming home after a long, arduous journey.

When their lips met it was with a sense of anticipation mingled with a deeper sense; this was exactly where they needed to be. After all this time and all Garret's journeys around the world, right now they were both in precisely the right place.

"THIS LOOKS REALLY GOOD." Pete stood in one of the bedrooms, his expression revealing more than his deadpan voice did.

Garret had to agree. Even though he, Larissa, Hailey, and Alanna had worked well into last night making up beds, hanging up pictures and putting finishing touches on the rooms and the hallway, the final transformation still surprised him.

"So what's your decision?" Garret asked, stifling his impatience with Pete. This was the fifth room they'd shown him.

"The carpet in the hallway still needs replacing," Pete said, tapping his pen against his lips. "You might want to look at some new light fixtures as well."

Garret sensed Pete was stalling. Maybe trying to get a better deal, but Garret wasn't budging.

So he said nothing.

Pete pulled out his phone and took another picture then turned back to Garret. "So the price you quoted is still in place?"

Garret nodded, crossing his arms over his chest letting his body language speak louder than his words.

"And we'll be able to book this entire block of rooms?" Pete asked.

"That's what we agreed on," Larissa put in, coming to stand beside Garret.

He caught a hint of her perfume as she lifted her arm to tuck her hair behind her ear. Her tiny gold earrings glinted in the light and with a start, Garret recognized them as a pair he had given her when they were dating. Promise earrings he had called them. A cheap imitation of all he wanted to give her and Larissa still had them.

He was surprised how good that made him feel, and how good she could make him feel. Since he had kissed her, he was constantly aware of her presence. Constantly looking for her, waiting for her, watching for her.

Each time they met as they got the rooms ready she would give him a shy smile. He would let his hand trail across her shoulder, down her back. Steal a kiss when he had a chance.

"So, we're not negotiating here?" Pete asked. "I got a pretty good price from the hotel in Highlands I was dealing with."

The numbers in the bank account made Garret hold his tongue. They were too deep into the operating loan to give anyone any deals. If he gave Pete a deal he'd have to give Renee from Scrap Happy a deal. The inn had to succeed on its own revenue. And if it couldn't...

Garret's thoughts slipped to the money he had tied up in investments. *Why not use that to pay the loan the inn was struggling to pay?*

What about your own plans for that money? Can you give up on that?

But that money had lost much of its value in the last drop in the market. If he pulled it out now he would lose way too much.

As the questions lingered, Larissa glanced up at him, her eyes meeting his, her mouth easing up in a smile of encouragement. As he held her gaze other questions rose up, overshadowing the first.

Why not put it all into this inn? Why not build a future here? With Larissa and the place she loves so much?

"Okay, I guess we'll do our conference here," Pete said, cutting off Garret's questions.

Larissa's hands flew to her mouth as she stifled a squeak of joy.

The tension holding Garret's shoulders melted away and he pulled Larissa close in an impulsive one-armed hug. "Excellent," he said, exhaling his concern. "You won't be sorry, Pete."

"I hope not," Pete said, one eyebrow rising as he looked at Larissa tucked up against Garret's side.

Garret didn't respond to the unspoken question in Pete's gaze, nor did he release Larissa. Instead he reached out his free hand to shake Pete's. "Thanks for your business. We'll be in touch," he said.

"Of course." Then Pete gave Larissa a wistful smile just as his phone rang. He held it up. "I need to take this call. I'll let myself out."

Garret felt he should accompany him, but Pete was already out the door, talking quickly in a subdued tone.

As soon as Pete was out of earshot, Garret turned to Larissa, caught her waist and swung her around. "We did it," he said, when he set her down, his grin almost splitting his face, surprised himself at the elation he felt at this victory. "We got Pete's conference."

Larissa pressed one hand to her chest, the other still clasping Garret's shoulder. "I thought for a moment he would change his mind," she said, her voice breathless. "I was trying not to be nervous so I just prayed. Hard."

Garret grinned down at her and then, bending over, pressed his lips to hers in a quick kiss of celebration. "You've been amazing through this all. It wouldn't have happened without all your work and organization."

Her smile lit up his heart.

"We did this together," she said. "You and me."

"I like the sound of that," he said, brushing another quick kiss over her lips as her words settled into his heart.

You and me.

Just like it should be.

He gave her a quick hug. "So, I guess we got work to do."

"I like the sound of that too." She trailed her fingers over his cheek. "You know what I liked the best about this?" she said her voice growing quiet as she rested her hand on his shoulder.

"Tell me," he encouraged.

"This was the first time, since I started managing the inn, that I've worked with someone who cares about it as much as I do." Her smile grew wistful. "I'm so glad you bought this inn. But I'm even happier that we're together...that we've been able to work together," she amended, a faint blush staining her cheeks.

Garret smiled at her obvious discomfort. "Are we together?" he asked, a teasing note entering his voice.

She looked down, but he tipped her chin up with this thumb and answered his own question with a slow, lingering kiss.

"I'd like to think we're together," he said. "Together again," he amended.

Her smile wavered a moment, as she focused her attention on her hand resting on his chest. "I just wish it hadn't taken so long. I missed you."

Her words tore at his heart and he pulled her close, cradling her head in his hand, brushing a light kiss over the top of her head.

"I missed you too," he said, feeling an unexpected twist of anger at the years that had kept them apart. "I thought of you so often."

She lay quiet a moment then said, "That day you came to the house...all those years ago...I'm sorry...I was so confused—"

Garret touched his finger to her lips, stopping her confession. He understood where she was coming from so much better now. "It doesn't matter anymore. You didn't know what had happened." Even as he spoke, Garret found his anger growing at her father and the lies that had come between them. "I've never cared about anyone as much as I cared about you," he said, keeping his voice even. She didn't need to know how he felt about her father. He was fairly sure she still didn't know what to think about the contrast in the stories he and her father had told.

To his surprise that didn't matter anymore. That misunderstanding belonged in a past where Larissa was young and impressionable. She was her own person now.

And after all this time, they were together.

He tilted her head up and kissed her again.

A sound at the door caught his attention. Was Pete back?

But when Larissa glanced over his shoulder, her smile shifted. Then she lowered her hand and stepped away from him.

Garret turned to see who or what had caused the change.

Jack Weir stood in the doorway, his dark eyes flitting from Garret to Larissa back to Garret again as if trying to determine what was going on. His tailored jacket lay in precise lines on his shoulders, framing the crisp blue shirt and perfectly knotted gray-and-blue striped silk tie. If Garret didn't know that only yesterday Jack had been clear across the Pacific Ocean, he would have guessed Larissa's father had just returned from a trip to his tailor.

Garret's heart slowed first, then began to race. The last time he saw Jack, he'd been standing in the imposing foyer of his home, Larissa between them, demanding that Garret leave. Demanding that Larissa come away from the door and come to him.

Jack looked as formidable as he had been back then.

In the silence that followed Jack's appearance, Garret's emotions veered from stunned shock to anger that surprised him in its ferocity.

After all these years there stood the man who had taken so much away from him. His mother's job, his own pride and, worst of all, the woman who now stood beside him, her face as pale as the white shirt she wore.

And how would Larissa react to her father's return?

TWELVE

"Hello, Dad," Larissa said, trying to get her head around the fact that her father was here, not Japan where he'd been the last time they spoke. "I thought you weren't coming back for a couple of days?"

"I completed my business early and thought I would surprise you. Clearly, I did." Her father shot a sidelong glance at Garret, then looked away, as if dismissing him. He walked up to Larissa and bent over to kiss her lightly on the cheek. "Hello, dear."

"Welcome back," she replied, happy to see him, yet unable to stifle a sense of guilt that he had caught her with Garret. "How was the trip? How did you get here from the airport? Why didn't you call?" She thought for sure, after an absence of a month, that he would at least want her to meet him at the airport.

"Baxter said you were busy, so he came and picked me up from the airport." Her father straightened and frowned as he looked around the room. "I see what you've been busy with."

"We did some painting and got some new bedding," Larissa

said, trying not to feel defensive about the simple changes they made. "We needed to do a quick, inexpensive overhaul of the top floor. We're getting ready for a conference that we just scored. The entire upper floor will be filled." She stopped herself there aware of how apologetic she sounded. As if what she and Garret had just accomplished was substandard instead of pretty amazing considering their timeline.

Jack looked around, his eyes taking it all in, his expression revealing nothing, but Larissa knew her father well enough to feel his disapproval. "Looks like a bed-and-breakfast. I wonder what your mother would think."

He spoke his words quietly, but they held a sardonic edge that hurt Larissa. Nothing about their achievement. Nothing about filling half of the inn—something that hadn't happened in the last three years.

"Thanks to Larissa's ideas and organization, we got the rooms painted and refurbished very quickly," Garret put in. "Because of that speedy turnaround, Pete Boonstra chose to have his conference here, which will be a huge boost in the arm for the inn's bottom line."

Larissa was grateful for Garret's support but at the same time disheartened at the terse note in his voice and at the narrowing of her father's eyes in response.

A sudden uptick of tension in the room caught her in its net. Why had her father decided to come back now when things were still so tentative between her and Garret?

Jack looked around the room again, the frown on his face creating an answering flush of irritation in Larissa. "I guess what's done is done," he said. Then he motioned to Garret. "We need to talk. Meet me downstairs in the office."

Larissa saw Garret stiffen at the overbearing tone in her father's voice. For a moment she wanted to remind her father that Garret was not his employee anymore. But years of obeying her father, letting him determine the course of her life, made her keep her comments to herself.

Garret glanced over at Larissa and flashed her a crooked smile as if to show her he didn't mind. Then he followed Jack out of the room.

As the door closed behind them, Larissa felt suddenly deflated and spent. Why did the sight of her father make her feel as if she'd been sneaking around behind his back?

She wasn't a child anymore. But as her father's eyes shot from her to Garret, she felt as if time had wheeled backward and again she was a young girl of eighteen and Garret the boyfriend her father didn't approve of.

She closed her eyes, trying to center herself. *Please, Lord,* she prayed, *help me to try to please You more than my father. Help me to take care of Garret and myself first.*

She waited a moment, as if to get her bearings.

Then she drew in a long, slow breath and strode out of the room and down the stairs. In spite of the tension of her father's unexpected return, she had a conference to get ready for.

GARRET CLOSED the door of the office, wishing he didn't feel so much like the teenager he used to be, sneaking around with the boss's daughter.

As Jack took his place behind the desk and Garret sat down across from him, Garret reminded himself that he had as much right to sit behind that desk as Larissa's father had. He wasn't Jack's employee. He was his partner.

He couldn't help remembering, however, the last time he and Jack were together as employer and employee when Jack had all the power.

Jack leaned back in the chair, unbuttoning his suit jacket,

looking across the desk at Garret. "So. This is an interesting turn of events," Jack was saying, his deep voice not even betraying the slightest hint of awkwardness.

Garret just nodded, deciding to let Jack determine the direction of this conversation. There were too many things he wanted to say to Jack but none of them would fall under the category of "business."

"I have to say I was stunned when I found out that Baxter sold his shares in this inn to you," Jack continued. "You were the last person I ever thought I would be partners with."

"I'm sure that was a surprise," Garret said, crossing his arms over his chest. Defensive body language, but it kept him from fidgeting.

Jack said nothing to that, as if waiting for Garret to explain how this happened. Garret was tempted to make some smart comment about turning a thousand dollars into a couple of hundred thousand, but he knew that would lead to a conversation about what Jack had told Larissa and he wasn't ready for that.

Jack eased out a sigh and leaned forward. "I also know you originally wanted to buy Baxter's share of the mill. I'm surprised you settled for this inn."

"Baxter changed his mind about selling," Garret replied. "He offered me this and I thought it would be a good opportunity."

"Six years ago it might have been," Jack said. "But a lot has changed since my wife's death..." He let the sentence trail off. The sorrow in his eyes created an answering thrum of sympathy in Garret. All history with Jack aside, Garret knew that he loved his wife.

"I was sorry for your loss," he said.

"Larissa told me you sent flowers." Jack tapped his fingers on the desktop. "She really appreciated that."

Garret again chose not to reply to the comment.

More finger tapping, then, "So what made you decide to come back? What made you decide to purchase this inn?"

Garret held Jack's intent gaze, taking his time to formulate his response. "I came back to keep a promise to my grandmother. Plus I wanted to settle in the community. Originally I thought I was buying Baxter's shares in the mill as you mentioned, but when this opportunity came up I took it."

"What part does my daughter play in this?"

He wanted to say that it was none of Jack's business. But because Larissa was Jack's daughter, that wasn't true. However, Garret wasn't one-hundred-percent sure where things were going with him and Larissa either. He knew he loved being with her. He knew that when he was with her his restlessness eased away. He also knew that in the past few weeks, as he spent time with her, he had been doing something he hadn't done since he left Rockyview.

He had started thinking about the future of his life instead of his bank account.

"I care a lot about your daughter," he said finally. "She's important to me and I believe she feels the same way." He stopped there, unwilling to expose too much of this fragile relationship too soon.

And he was also afraid that if he said too much, he wouldn't be able to contain his simmering anger.

"You don't like me, do you?" Jack threw the question down like a challenge, obviously picking up on what Garret had tried so hard to suppress.

Garret waited a beat, unsure of how to respond to this direct question. "Is that important to you?" he asked instead.

Jack curled his one hand into a fist, then uncurled it again. "If you and my daughter are getting involved again, then I guess it factors in."

Involved again. Those seemingly innocuous words quickly dredged up all the resentment that had built since Larissa told Garret about the money Jack had supposedly given him. Garret quashed the feeling, struggling to relegate it to the past where it belonged.

But he knew that as long as his and Larissa's relationship was going the way it was, he would have to have that conversation with Jack sometime.

Then his cell phone buzzed and he pulled it out of his pocket, glancing at the display. Benny Alpern.

"I'm sorry, I should take this call." He didn't really have to, but he was thankful for the diversion. "Unless there's something else you need to discuss?"

Jack shook his head and sat back in the chair. "Take the call. We'll need to go over a few things later on, though."

Garret nodded, as he got to his feet. He waited until he was outside the office to answer the muted call.

"Benny, what can I do for you?" he asked as he closed the office door behind him.

"The check you wrote me bounced."

Garret frowned at the blunt pronouncement. "What? How could that happen?" Though they were reaching the bottom end of the operating loan, there was still a few thousand left in it. He knew that.

"I brought it to the bank. I got it back. Insufficient funds. That's how it happened," Benny snapped.

"Okay. I'll look into this right away," Garret said. "Sorry about that. You'll get your money."

"I better. I got bills to pay too, you know."

"Of course you do."

Garret managed to placate Benny, then hung up just as Larissa came down the stairs. As soon as she saw him, she hurried over, glancing at the office doors behind him.

"So, what did my dad want?" Concern edged her voice and pulled her brows together in a frown.

"Just to touch base."

Larissa's frown deepened, as if Garret's answer didn't satisfy her. "You look upset. What did he say to make you angry?"

Garret shook his head and gave her shoulder a quick squeeze of assurance. "I'm upset because Benny Alpern just told me his check bounced."

"What? We had enough money to cover that." Larissa bit her lip, then shot Garret a horrified look. "If Benny's check bounced, that means we won't have enough to cover the credit card bill."

"I'll look into it," Garret said, not wanting to bring up what he'd been pushing for lately. Online access to the bank accounts for himself and Larissa. Everyone agreed it should happen but with Larissa's father gone and Orest stalling it hadn't happened yet. It didn't seem a big deal.

Until now.

Larissa looked back at the office door. "So are you and my dad okay?"

"We're okay," he said with forced cheer. But behind his smile, thoughts and concerns festered.

Now that her dad was back, how would that affect their relationship?

"DON'T DROP THAT PLATE NOW."

Shannon's quiet voice broke into Garret's wandering thoughts.

"Sorry, I was just thinking," he said, giving his cousin a quick smile.

"Surprised you can above this noise," Shannon said, setting another dripping plate on the drainboard between them.

Olivia and Natasha were playing an overly loud game of Go Fish in the dining room to the left of the kitchen and from the living room around the corner, boisterous conversation punctuated with the occasional laugh from Hailey floated back to them.

Shannon and Hailey's sister Naomi had returned to Rockyview yesterday and the family was circling the wagons around her, determined to make her transition back into family life and town life as easy as possible. Hence the dinner at Nana Bond's.

Larissa had asked if Garret wanted to come with her for a walk up Hartley Pass, but he had to beg off, because of Naomi. Larissa understood and for a moment he'd been tempted to ask her to come here.

But at the last moment, he stalled out. Taking her to a Bond family get-together just seemed to be pushing things too quickly. Too public a declaration.

Besides, Hailey and Shannon would be all over him with questions and ideas and advice. Not what he needed right now.

Garret gave the plate he still held on to a quick wipe with his tea towel just in case he'd missed something, thankful he hadn't given in to the impulse.

"The inn still going strong?" Shannon asked.

"Stumbling along," he said, pulling his attention back to his cousin. "But we have Pete Boonstra's conference this week and that will help. The dining room is starting to turn a real profit so, yeah, we're moving toward strong. I hope." He tried not to think about Benny Alpern's bounced check. They would deal with that the next time they met with Orest.

"You sound doubtful."

Garret wiped a mug, wishing he knew exactly what to say

and how to say it. He'd been on his own so long, he had forgotten how to share what he was thinking.

Thankfully Shannon just kept working, letting the rhythm of something as simple as doing the dinner dishes ease the awkwardness of the moment.

"I'm starting to think about my future," Garret finally said as he wiped the last of the glasses.

"I thought that was the reason you came back here. To settle down and build your future here." Shannon lifted her shoulder and wiped away a few errant bubbles that had landed on her cheek as she drained the water from the sink.

"It was. Still is. But I came with different ideas and plans." Garret set the last glass into the cupboard above the counter, tossed the tea towel over his shoulder and leaned back against the counter. "I wanted to show Rockyview what I was made of. To come back a man of substance."

Shannon brushed her wavy hair back from her face and leaned against the counter as well, unconsciously mimicking Garret's stance.

"You're part owner of an inn. I think that gives you some substance."

Garret laughed. "It does I guess. Though I wouldn't enjoy it near as much if it weren't for Larissa."

"You sound doubtful."

Garret sighed, wishing he knew exactly how to articulate the reshaping of his emotions, plans and priorities.

"I've always been the kind of guy who makes a plan and sticks with it," he said, shoving his hands into the pockets of his pants. "I've never had second thoughts. But lately..." He let his voice trail off. "Lately all I can think about is creating the kind of life I can be proud of. A life that will allow me to take care of..." He hesitated, his feelings for Larissa, though changing and growing, still almost too sacred and special to articulate.

"To take care of Larissa in the manner to which she is accustomed?" Shannon finished for him.

Garret chuckled at the old-fashioned phrasing. "Yeah. I guess that's it. You know what her parents' house looks like. It's a mansion."

"So. Do you think that matters to her?"

Garret thought of the differences of opinion they had on the renovations at the inn. How she wanted to do things right. The money she was willing to spend. He was still surprised she had been willing to settle for bargain linens from a small-time store.

"I'm hoping it won't."

"I don't think she's the kind of person who cares how much money she has in her bank account as long as she is with someone who loves her," Shannon said, a faint tone of censure in her voice.

"That sounds all noble and good," Garret said, a faintly harsh note entering his voice. "But you and I both lived with the results of being broke and not having enough. It's humiliating and it's not fun. I wouldn't wish that on my future wife and children."

"I still believe that if you're with a person who loves you then money isn't as important as you seem to think it is."

Garret thought again of the inn's balance sheet and how long it would be, even with Pete's and Rene's business, before the inn showed the kind of profit he knew the mill would.

"I can tell you're still not sure."

"I'm trying to reconcile what I want for her and what I'm able to give her. If I stay the owner of the inn, I don't know if I can support her."

"The inn is supporting her now," Shannon said.

"I suppose," he conceded, thinking of the salary Larissa was pulling from the inn. It was a reasonable sum, but it wasn't a huge amount.

"Remember the story of August that Nana loves to tell us?"

Garret nodded, smiling as he thought of the necklace and Bible his grandmother had given him when he came here.

"August made choices too. At first, he made the wrong ones. He chose to chase the illusion of wealth. But he realized what a mistake he made and he came back to Nukinu. Which is a good thing because otherwise you and I wouldn't be here to have this conversation," Shannon said with a laugh. "But he knew he made the right choice. In the end, even though it would have made a difference for them, they didn't do anything with those gold nuggets either, did they?"

Garret laughed at that. "No. I guess they didn't."

Shannon lifted the nugget on her necklace, looking down at it. "And neither did we." She smiled, then tucked the nugget back into her shirt, looking back at Garret. "When Ben asked me to marry him, the last thing, the very last thing on my mind, was how he would support me or how we would live."

"Considering he's a doctor and you're a nurse, that was a no-brainer," Garret joked.

Shannon smacked him lightly on the shoulder. "It wasn't even a blip on the radar, mister. Even now, as we're trying to find a place to live, what matters more to me is the home we're going to make, rather than the house we might be living in." Shannon stepped closer to him and rested her hand on his shoulder. "You have to let go of your ideas of what success is. You have to recognize that making a success of a relationship is far, far more important than making a success of your life. Wasn't it Emerson who said that laughing often and winning the respect of intelligent people and the affection of children and leaving the world a better place because you lived was his definition of success?" She clapped her hands.

"I guess, as a Christian, I would add that to know you loved God and loved the people around you more than you loved yourself would define you as a success. At least in my eyes and I know, for sure, in Nana's eyes as well." Shannon patted his shoulder then stepped back. "I see how Larissa looks at you. It's the same one that I see when Hailey looks at Dan, when Sabine looks at Tanner. Give Larissa credit for caring for you—enough that to her it doesn't matter how much money you have as long as you love her."

Garret let Shannon's words rest on his heart and stifle his second thoughts.

He knew Larissa cared for him.

Yes, things were changing between them and he knew his feelings were stronger now than all those years ago. He dared to make plans. To look into a future with Larissa, working at the inn. Making it the success he wanted his life to be.

He just wished he believed it was enough.

THIRTEEN

"I didn't think it would come together, man." Pete Boonstra took a sip of his coffee as he looked around the packed dining room of laughing, cheerful real estate agents. "You worked a miracle here."

"You underestimate Larissa's organizational abilities," Garret said, catching a glimpse of Larissa as she gently steered a young server toward a group of people. She glanced around the room, her lips puckered and a gentle frown marring her beautiful face. Watching, making sure everything was running as it had all week. Like clockwork. Then she caught him looking her way and her frown faded, the pucker turned into a smile and she waggled her fingers at him.

Since the forty people registered for the conference had descended on the inn, he and Larissa hadn't managed more than a passing glance, a stolen kiss in the office, a quick touch as they passed each other in the hallway.

Garret had taken his family up on their offer and Hailey, Dan, Tanner, Shannon, and Ben had helped him clean up the grounds even as people were arriving.

Garret could still smile at the memory of his cousins and brother mowing, clipping, bagging and chiding each other as they scurried along. He still felt guilty about asking them to help when they'd done so much already, but he was told, in no uncertain terms by both his brother and Hailey, that this is what family does.

The thought had humbled him. He'd been away from family so long he didn't think he deserved all the support and help he'd received.

From here, standing by the French doors leading to the patio, he saw the amazing results of their work. The grounds had regained their parklike appearance and a semblance of their former glory.

And for the first time since he had reluctantly bought into this inn he felt as if he could breathe easier. It would work out, he thought, glancing across the room and catching Larissa's eye again.

He missed having quality time with her, and the thought put an ache in his heart.

"Excuse me, Pete," he said, putting down his coffee cup on the sideboard. He skirted the edges of the room, not making eye contact, hoping he wouldn't be waylaid.

However, he wasn't sneaky enough. One tall, lanky fellow caught him by the arm as he passed and pulled him against his will, into their conversation. "Say, Bond. I love what you did with the place," the man was saying. His name badge said that he was Horace Hockstein. *Not the most auspicious name for a real estate agent,* Garret thought. "You've got lots of potential here. Lots that can be done. Pete was telling me you're thinking of subdividing the property? Possibly flipping it? If you do, let me know. This is prime real estate."

Garret frowned, wondering where Pete had gotten the idea

and why he told Horace, but before he had a chance to correct the man, he saw Larissa coming out of the kitchen.

She handed a full tray of canapés to another server, stopped to straighten a flower arrangement and then looked up.

He kept his eyes on her as he walked toward her, giving only a quick smile to another person who called out his name. He made it to her side without any further distractions and took her arm.

"Come with me," he said, giving her a quick smile. "I think we both need some fresh air."

"I just have to fill another tray," she said. "Then I'll come."

"Emily and the servers can take care of that," he said, gently pulling her along. She protested, but let him lead her out of the dining room and into the foyer.

A group of people stood by the fireplace, holding forth about the changing real estate market, so he kept on going.

"What do you need me to see?" she asked.

"Trust me." Garret opened the front door and a wave of cool evening air washed into the inn. He led her out into the gathering dusk, down the flagstone path, then he veered to the right and there it was. An arbor once overgrown by ivy, now clipped and neat. And tucked in the arbor was a rustic wooden bench that Hailey had found behind the gardening shed.

"Oh, my goodness," Larissa said, her voice breathless as Garret pulled her down on the bench beside him, her eyes shining, her fingers pressed to her cheek in surprise. "I can't believe you got all this done. I remember when my mother put up this arbor. I've been wanting to get the ivy tamed...and oh, my, the ramble. It looks so much better as well." She pointed to a maze of shrubs and trees with another flagstone path meandering through. "This is amazing. I can't believe you got all this done so quickly." The pleasure and pride in her voice made all the late nights and stress worthwhile. Much work still needed to be done, but Garret felt a sense of pride and accomplishment at what had already been done.

"The place is starting to look really good," he said settling back onto the bench, his arm around Larissa as he looked over the property. *His property*, he thought, his arm tightening around her shoulders. *His and Larissa's.*

The thought landed and took root. He thought of what Shannon had told him this past Sunday and he allowed himself to indulge in the possibilities of a future with Larissa.

He turned to her, a sense of rightness lowering into his soul. "You know, this is the first time in my life that I've owned anything resembling a home."

"Really? You've never owned property before?" Astonishment crept over her face and tinged her voice.

"No. I've been on the move so much, it was never worth it."

"But this inn isn't really a home," she said quietly.

"Maybe not, but it's the closest I've come."

She was quiet a moment as unspoken feelings drifted around them, waiting to be expressed.

Garret wasn't sure what more to say. He felt as if he were standing at a crossroads in his life. As he looked down at Larissa, he wondered if he dared to take the next step. And if he did, would she come along? Would it be enough for her?

"I'm so glad you bought out my uncle's share of the inn," Larissa said, laying her head against Garret's shoulder. "My dad was never interested in this inn, Uncle Baxter was just a silent partner. But since you came on board, I feel like I finally have someone working with me who gets it. Who understands." She shifted so she could look up at him. "I'm so glad you're my partner."

"I am, too," he said, a sense of well-being and completeness filling him. Then he tipped her face up to his and kissed her forehead. Then he rained light kisses on her cheek moving his way to her mouth.

They shared a kiss that lengthened and deepened and made his heart beat harder.

She was so precious. So beautiful. So loving.

"I had another reason to take you out here," he said. "I was wondering if you want to go out with me tomorrow night. For dinner."

"That sounds wonderful," Larissa said with a smile that made him want to kiss her again.

"I know the food is great here, but I thought a change of scenery was in order and I want to celebrate the success of this conference."

"It went well, didn't it?"

"You were amazing," he said. He brushed his fingers over her cheek.

"Larissa?"

Her father's voice broke into the moment. Jack came around the corner a dark figure, the light from the inn casting him in shadow. Garret had to fight the urge to pull back and hide.

He shook the feeling off, angry that Jack could still have this effect on him. He had nothing to be ashamed of and he had nothing to apologize for.

"I'm over here, Dad." Larissa got to her feet and Garret followed suit, feeling once again like a kid caught with his hand in the cookie jar. "Garret and I were just taking a break."

"I see that," her father said with a sardonic lift of his eyebrow. Then he released a sigh, shooting a quick glance over his shoulder. "Emily asked where you were. I said I would go looking for you."

"Did she say what she needed?"

"It wasn't important." Jack was silent a moment and Garret

stopped himself from trying to fill the silence. "Looks like the conference went well," Jack continued.

"Larissa did a lot of work." Garret tried not to react to the surprise in Jack's voice. "She's been working very hard the past few days."

"You've done a lot too," Larissa protested. "Have you seen the grounds? They look amazing. Garret's been working on them ever since he came here."

"I got a lot of help from my family."

"That's good. I'm sure it helped."

Then to Garret's surprise, Jack gave them both a quick smile. "I'm heading home right now, will you be coming later?" he asked, turning to Larissa.

"When I'm done here," she said.

Jack nodded, then without another word walked past them both to his car. As he got in and drove away, Garret couldn't help notice the make and model of the vehicle.

A little out of his league. No, make that a lot out of his league.

Then he pushed the thought aside. What Jack drove and how much money he had shouldn't matter.

But even as he and Larissa walked into the inn, he couldn't help realize the vehicle Jack drove cost as much as Garret used to make in a year.

Don't go there, he reminded himself. *You're not Jack Weir.*

But he couldn't stop the faint niggle of concern that always dogged him when he and Larissa were dating. Could he really give her all she needed knowing what she grew up with?

As the inn doors closed behind them, Larissa turned to Garret, laying a gentle arm on his. "I need to talk to Emily. Can you make sure things are rolling smoothly at the reception?"

"Of course," Garret said. "Let me know if you need me," he said.

Then she gave him another quick smile and left. He watched her leave, smiling at the bounce in her step and the way her hair shone in the overhead lights.

Lights that would need to be replaced soon, he realized with a sense of dismay. And the carpet of the stairs should be taken care of. The other day he noticed that some of the seals had broken on a few of the windows.

Tomorrow, he reminded himself. *That's for tomorrow.* For tonight he wanted to revel in the success of the conference and the promise of a better future.

What exactly that would look like, he wasn't entirely sure. But for now, for the first time in his life he felt as if he was exactly where he was supposed to be.

"I DON'T UNDERSTAND," Larissa said, tapping her pen on the table as she glanced from Orest to Garret. "The conference did so well. I thought we'd be further along financially than we are."

Orest lifted one thin shoulder as he adjusted his glasses. "I'm sorry, but the numbers don't lie."

Larissa pulled her lower lip between her teeth, feeling a twist in the pit of her stomach as she saw the final numbers on the monthly balance sheet.

"Is this why Benny's check bounced?" Garret asked, his arms folded on the table as he scowled at the papers lying in front of him.

"Benny?" Orest frowned.

"Alpern. The fellow who did the painting for us at the inn."

Orest frowned and shuffled through some more of the papers as if looking for the elusive Benny.

"I got a call from him, telling me that his check bounced," Garret said. "I thought we had enough to cover it."

"Obviously not," Orest said, blinking as he removed his glasses. He gave Larissa a tight-lipped smile. "You were fairly deep into the operating loan, I might add."

"But the conference...we did so well." Larissa shook her head in puzzlement.

"There were extra costs you didn't anticipate which made you overdrawn." He fiddled with his watch, adjusted the papers on the desk and put his glasses on again.

Larissa fought down a twinge of annoyance. Orest was always a nervous sort. Today he seemed worse. She could hardly blame him. Being the bearer of bad news was never easy.

Garret pushed the papers away as if he didn't want to look at them anymore. "I can't believe these numbers. You must have made a mistake."

Orest rubbed the side of his nose with his finger as he shook his head. "I'm a Chartered Accountant. I don't make mistakes."

Garret said nothing and the silence in the office seemed fraught with tension. Larissa hunched her shoulders as she looked down at the numbers again, but she couldn't change the reality. The conference that was supposed to save the inn hadn't.

Then the door opened, letting in the chatter from guests checking in at the lobby. Early birds for the scrapbooking conference, Larissa thought. In half an hour she would be meeting with Renee to go over some of the last minute venue changes for the extra guests that had arrived. Word of mouth from Pete's conference had been positive and Renee had to deal with a few more people from Rockyview who suddenly wanted to stay at the inn as well. Things should be looking up.

But they weren't.

"What did I miss?" Jack Weir said, as he closed the door on the noise and came and sat at the table.

"We were just going over the monthly financial statement," Larissa said.

"How are things looking?"

Larissa sighed. "Not as good as we had hoped."

"I'm having a hard time believing that conference didn't make more money than this balance sheet shows," Garret said, leaning back in his chair, tapping his fingers on the armrests. "There's a mistake somewhere. Has to be."

"What are you implying?" Jack asked with a frown.

Garret leaned forward, his hands resting on the table. "I'm implying my concern. And I want to say again that we need to have an external audit done on the books and I'd like the bank account to be made available online so that Larissa, you, and I can access it anytime we need to."

"What do you think about that?" Jack said, turning to Orest.

Larissa wasn't surprised to see him straighten, his head up, looking directly at her father.

And avoiding looking at her and Garret.

"I'm working on getting the bank account online. I prefer to pay the bills with checks, however. I prefer a paper trail."

"Any problem with that?" Her father quirked a questioning eyebrow toward Larissa.

"I have a problem with it," Garret said, his tone firm. "We are the owners and partners of this business and need access to all the information we can get. Besides, it's archaic."

"Archaic?" was all Jack said, the one word holding many implications.

"And the audit?" Garret pressed. "That's even more important."

Jack frowned just as Orest interjected. "That's not necessary."

"Why is this a problem?" Larissa asked, puzzled at Orest's continuing resistance.

"We'll deal with this later," her father said, shooting a warning glance at Larissa as if reminding her of her place.

Larissa held his gaze. For a moment she was tempted to back down, wondering herself why this was necessary. It would just cause hard feelings.

Except Garret thought it was important. And it was.

She looked from her father to Garret, her mind ticking back over all the work Garret had done and was still doing for the inn. How many evenings had she heard the mower going or seen him hauling bags of leaves and weeds he had raked and pulled up?

She thought of the consulting they had done for Pete's conference, the painting, the shopping.

Garret had been a true partner in every sense of the word while her father, in all the years he'd had ownership of the inn had never done half of what Garret had.

So who had more right to make a few demands?

Then Larissa heard Garret's sigh and she felt her own resolve stiffen. "Why not talk about it now? We're all here." Larissa ignored Orest's pained look and instead looked at her father directly. "Having the audit done is a business decision. Plain and simple."

Orest's face blanched and he turned to her father. "Jack, I have done nothing that needs to be examined."

"Larissa, I can't believe you're doing this," her father protested. "Orest has been a long-standing staff member. Faithful and dependable. He's an old friend of the family. This makes it look like you don't trust him."

Larissa looked at Orest, his dear familiar face and for a

moment felt her resolve wavering. Could it be that Garret was wrong? After all, he said he wasn't a bookkeeper.

At the same time, even if everything was on the up-and-up, wouldn't it be a good idea to have this done? And then she looked at Garret who gave her a slight nod, as if encouraging her.

She took a deep breath and then looked at Orest, avoiding her father's gaze. "This isn't anything personal. We're not trying to besmirch your character, Orest, but I believe this has to be done."

"You don't have that kind of authority," her father blustered. "You're not a partner in this inn. You only hold a two percent share."

Larissa's heart turned over at her father's bald comment. Though part of her knew it was true, she felt as if he had put her into her place. A very small, two percent place.

"But her share is important," Garret was saying. "You and I don't agree on this matter. So her share tips the balance."

Her father's irate gaze ticked over Garret. "What are you saying?"

"I'm saying that right now Larissa holds all the cards. I want the audit. You don't." Garret turned back to Larissa. "It's your call, Larissa. You make the decision."

Her father frowned, obviously uncomfortable with this turn of events. "I already said I don't want to discuss this further," Jack said. "Orest. Garret. If you'll give me a moment with my daughter," he asked.

Garret was about to stand up when Larissa put her hand on his arm to stop him. "There's nothing more to discuss," Larissa continued, feeling a sudden and exhilarating sense of freedom. And, she had to admit, power. "Garret and I both want the audit done. I'm not changing my mind on this."

Her father folded his arms over his chest as he held Larissa's gaze. "You're really siding with Garret?"

Larissa looked from Garret to her father and though her heart was pounding so hard she thought it would burst through her chest, she felt a smile pull at her mouth.

"I'm not siding with anyone. I'm making my own choice for the good of the inn," she said, her voice quiet and surprisingly calm considering her heart was beating like a bass drum. But as she drew in a ragged breath, and another, slowly she felt a deep sense of peace come over her.

Her father kept his gaze on her, but she didn't back down and then she felt Garret's hand brush her back. A gentle touch but it warmed her soul and kept her from looking away from her father's piercing gaze.

Then Jack slapped his hands on the table. "Then I guess this is how it will have to be but I want you to know that I don't like it."

"Duly noted," Larissa said, experiencing a surprising adrenaline rush over her victory. And for the first time in her life she felt as if she was her own person.

"Is there anything else that needs to be covered?" her father asked as he glanced at his watch. "I'm meeting Baxter at the mill in half an hour."

"Not much more to talk about," Garret said, his hand still resting on Larissa's back.

Orest got up, rearranging the papers on the table and then shoved them in his briefcase. He looked across the table at Larissa, his expression pained, as if she had just kicked him.

"I'm sorry you feel the need to do this," he said, sorrow edging his voice.

"And I'm sorry this is such a problem for you," Larissa said. "It doesn't mean we don't trust you. It's not personal at all."

Orest shook his head, as if he didn't believe her. Then he followed Jack out of the office.

The clicking of the door was followed by a moment of silence and then Larissa turned to Garret, a few doubts snaking their way up her resolve.

"We did the right thing, didn't we?"

"*You* did the right thing," he said, giving her an encouraging smile. "It was all up to you. But you know that I support your decision and I'm proud of you."

Larissa's smile broadened and she felt as if all the twists and turns of her life had brought her to this place.

And it was a good place.

"Things will work out, you know?" she said, touching his cheek, stroking an errant strand of hair back from his forehead.

Garret nodded, but Larissa saw a tightness around his mouth that was new.

"Is something wrong?"

He glanced at the papers on the table and sighed. "I'm glad we're getting an audit done, but it doesn't change a really important fact." He looked back at her. "Unless things change drastically in the next couple of weeks, we'll have a tough time paying the regular bills."

His words were like a chill in the office. She tried to shake the reality off.

"It will work out," she said, placing her hand on his shoulder. "I know it will."

He gave her a crooked smile. "I'm glad you're so full of optimism."

"Why shouldn't I be? I have a great partner who has a great vision."

He just laughed at that, gave her another quick kiss and then left.

But as he did, some of the warmth left the room as well.

Larissa hugged herself and walked to the window, trying not to think about what Garret had just said.

Just outside the window she saw a young couple walking down one of the paths, then disappear around the bend. Two younger women stood on the bridge, taking pictures of each other. A group of older men stood in the parking lot, laughing, chattering.

Everyone looked so happy. And they were happy because they were here.

Unless things change drastically...

Garret's words resounded through her head and she laid her forehead against the cool glass of the window. Were things really that dire that they wouldn't be able to meet their financial obligations?

She didn't want to think about what that could mean. All she ever wanted to do was run this inn. It was her legacy to her mother. Now Garret was back in her life and together they were working on her dream.

It was as if all the things she had ever wanted were now coming together.

Dear Lord, she prayed. *Help me to trust that whatever happens will happen for the best. Help me to know what to hold on to and what to let go of.*

And she didn't want to think too hard about what that might entail.

FOURTEEN

"So what did you want to talk about?" Garret folded his arms over his chest, his wooden chair creaking as he leaned back, staring hard at his steaming cup of coffee. Trying not to wonder too hard why Jack wanted to meet at Mug Shots instead of at the inn.

When Jack had called him last night with a request to meet him early this morning, Garret had asked why. Jack had simply said he didn't want to have this conversation in front of Larissa.

Now Garret sat across from Jack in the back corner of the café, a bit removed from the usual chatter of people coming and going. The scent of bread baking wafted through the room, counterpointed by the ever-present smell of coffee.

Smelled like home, Garret thought.

Jack tugged on the cuffs of his shirt, then rested his arms on the table, hands stacked one over the other. "I may as well come right to the point. I want to buy your share of the inn."

Garret heard the words but it seemed to take a few more moments for them to register. "Why do you want to do that?" According to Larissa her father wasn't that interested in the inn, so why would he want full ownership? It didn't make sense.

"I have a few plans I want to capitalize on and in order to do that, I will need majority ownership of the inn." Jack leaned forward, his chair creaking as his eyes held Garret's. "I know that the inn wasn't your first choice. I know you bought it from Baxter for the express purpose of flipping it."

Garret held Jack look for look, trying not to let the man intimidate him. "Yes. That was my original plan," he said. No need to hide that fact. "But things have changed for me."

"I take it one of those 'things'—" Jack lifted his forefingers making air quotes "—is your renewed relationship with my daughter."

Garret didn't like Jack's tone of voice, but chose to ignore it. "Yes. My relationship with Larissa is a factor. Plus I've found I really enjoy working at the inn and I really enjoy working with Larissa. She has a real heart for the place and has helped me to see it as more than just a business."

Jack nodded, as if he understood what Garret was saying. "Her mother felt the same way before she got ill."

In spite of the history between them, Garret couldn't help a flicker of sympathy for the man. From what he remembered about Larissa's parents, they did love each other deeply.

Then Jack folded his hands together and dropped them on the table, as if putting an end to the reverie. "But we need to move on and, for me, that means purchasing your share of the inn."

Jack seemed adamant, which made Garret curious.

"Why do you want to do that?"

"Baxter is finally willing to sell his share of the mill. I need to finance my purchase of that."

A strange sense of déjà vu washed over Garret as he took a quick sip of his coffee. A few weeks ago he had come to this very place to do exactly what Jack was talking about. Buy out Baxter's shares in the mill.

Garret felt a bite of irritation that Baxter hadn't approached him about selling his shares as he had promised. Even as the thought grew right behind it came another question.

Is that really what you want?

"How would purchasing my share of the inn help you finance buying out Baxter?" he asked, keeping his focus on the topic at hand. If Baxter was selling his shares, Jack would be the logical purchaser anyhow.

"I want to sell the inn and I can't do that if I only own forty-nine percent."

His bald statement was like a body blow.

In his dealings with various petroleum companies, Garret had been party to a number of business deals and takeovers. But never as an owner.

Now he understood why even some hard-nosed busi-nessman could blanch and recoil at the thought of their busi-ness being dismantled and sold. And by one of the owner's relatives.

His heart broke for Larissa.

"You'd really sell the place?"

"It hasn't meant anything to me since my wife died and I can't believe it means anything to you."

At one time it didn't, but Garret's involvement in the inn had changed him. Had made him part of a community. As he had told Larissa, for the first time in his life he felt as if he was truly rooted in a place and had an investment in seeing it succeed.

But was it succeeding?

"You and I both know how precarious the financial situa-tion of the inn is," Jack continued, as if sensing Garret's hesitation. "If you sell it to me, you'll at least recoup some of your investment."

Jack's words were like a cold dash of reality that only underlined Garret's own misgivings. All the hopes Garret had pinned on the conference had been dashed. The inn wasn't coming around as he and Larissa had hoped.

"But Larissa...what will she do if you sell it? This inn is her life."

"This inn has sucked too much out of her already. It's time she put it behind her and moved on with her life. This was not what I had planned for my daughter."

Garret was surprised at the bitter tone that had crept into Jack's voice. As if he resented the place the inn had taken in her life and for a moment he wondered if Jack had felt the same way about his wife's involvement in the inn.

"I know the inn didn't do as well after Pete's conference as I had hoped," Garret said, holding on to his gut feeling that this inn could make it. "I'm still optimistic we can turn this place around."

"Garret. Be logical. You know how the financials look. You'll have to have twenty conferences like Pete's before you can even begin to pay back the operating loan. And how feasible is that in a town the size of Rockyview?"

Garret pressed his lips together, trying not to let Jack's reasonable tone get to him. "Once Albert has finished his audit, I am sure we'll be able to come up with a solution to the financial problems of the inn. At one time it made money. It can again."

"Maybe, but will it be enough for you to take care of Larissa?"

There it was again. The idea that Garret was unable to provide for his beloved daughter. That he would never be able to make enough to keep her in the manner to which she was accustomed. As if Larissa was a child who

"I have my own money yet," Garret snapped. "I'm not the broke laborer who wasn't good enough for your daughter. I'm not the guy you told your daughter was willing to leave her for a measly ten thousand dollars." As soon as he spoke the words he wished he could take them back. This was not what he was here to talk about.

Jack sat back, his features tightening at Garret's accusation. "What are you talking about?"

"I think you know." Garret leaned forward as if to press his point home. "Why did you tell Larissa you gave me ten thousand dollars when we both knew it was only a grand which covered my wages and some holiday pay? Why did you convince her it was some kind of payout?" The questions burst out on a wave of anger and as soon as they came out, Garret pressed his lips together as if to prevent further outbursts. He was crazy to bring up the past like that. What did it matter anymore? He and Larissa were together now.

Jack sat back, sucking in a quick breath. "She told you, did she?"

Garret's only response was a tight nod.

Jack rubbed his hand over his chin, but then he lowered it and his eyes were unapologetic. "I had to. I had to protect my little girl."

"From what?"

Jack waited a moment, his gaze steady and uncompromising. "From you. From getting involved with someone who wouldn't be able to give her a good life."

Jack's words were so close to the ones Garret had repeated to himself as he left town, that Garret felt his heart turn over.

"How did you manage to convince her of the amount? She said you showed her the check."

"A simple matter of adding a zero in the amount and changing a word."

Garret stared at him, stunned that he would resort to deception all in an effort to protect Larissa from him.

Didn't you feel the same way?

"All I've ever done has been for Larissa," Jack said. "I let her play around with this inn because it's what she loves to do. It was her way of staying connected to her mother. But the longer she runs it, the longer you both run it, the more equity you burn up, the more money you'll lose. Let me buy it from you and you can do something else."

Garret looked away from Jack and his oh-so-reasonable arguments to the window overlooking the valley. He saw the mountain where the Shadow Woman was just starting to show herself. His mind didn't want to acknowledge what Jack was telling him.

If he sold the inn what would he do? He was starting to make plans for a life with Larissa. He and Larissa were building dreams around their plans to make the inn a retreat. A place where, as Larissa had said, people find rest. Peace.

The same peace he had found. Working outside on the grounds nourished a part of his inner being that had lain fallow since he left the ranch. When he was outside, it was as if he could feel God's touch on his soul.

He didn't want to lose that.

He turned back to Jack, shaking his head, negating Jack's seemingly levelheaded comments.

"I can't do that to Larissa," he said. "And I don't want to do it to myself. I am convinced we can make this inn profitable. I'll know more once we get the external audit done."

"The audit won't show you anything different from what Orest can show you."

"Probably not, but I asked Albert to give us a financial plan that might give us some direction. Something Orest seems reluctant to do." Garret dragged his hand over his face. "We just need to do something different, that's all. Take a different tack. Take some risks. Try something new." He stopped himself there, hating the note of desperation that had crept into his voice. While part of him was confident in the inn's potential, his rational self wondered if he was getting distracted by his feelings for Larissa. And her feelings for this inn.

He thought of the money he still had invested. Money that had dropped to half of its former value in the past six months. Did he dare pull it now and put it into a business that couldn't seem to hold its own? Would he be smart to cut his losses, sell his share of the inn to Jack, wait for his investments to improve and purchase a more successful business?

The thoughts spun around in the silence that followed his overly confident declaration to Jack.

Jack said nothing for a long while, as if he too, sensed that Garret was overcompensating. Then he looked up at Garret. "You haven't been taking much of a wage from the inn."

Garret heard the unspoken reproach in Jack's voice and he felt his back stiffen. *Here we go again,* he thought. *Still not able to support his daughter.* "I pull enough to live on. The same amount Larissa does." Which was his way of saying that what he lived on, Larissa could, too.

Jack shook his head slowly, back and forth, then sighed. "Larissa has money coming in from a trust fund established by her grandparents. Paula's parents. She's had that since she first took over the inn. That's the only way she's been able to work there and live off what she's pulling out of the inn in wages."

Garret looked at Jack, his words slowly sinking in. "Larissa never told me about this."

"And why would she? She probably didn't want you to know."

Garret felt his own hopes sink. How could he have been so foolish? Larissa wasn't living comfortably on her wages from the inn. Of course she wasn't. She was used to a better life.

"So, what's your answer?" Jack asked.

Garret shook his head. "I need time to think about this." He had to get his head around what Jack had just told him.

Had to figure out which was the practical solution and which was him trying to live out some foolish dream of running the inn with Larissa and making a living doing it.

"Baxter said he would give me an exclusive deal but only for the next four days," Jack continued. "I need to have an answer before Monday."

Four days? How could he figure out what he needed to do in such a short time frame?

But he had no choice. He had to make a decision. He just wished he had more time to do it.

LARISSA HUNG up the phone and checked off another tedious task from her to-do list. She had ensconced herself in the office, dealing with some final reckonings on the bills from the scrapbooking conference that was winding down today.

The door of the office opened and she glanced up. Garret. Her heart did that funny little jump it always did when she saw him.

He closed the door then leaned back, his head dropping against the door, seemingly unaware she was there. He stayed that way a moment, before pushing away. He pulled back, as if startled, his frown deepening when he saw her.

"Is something wrong?" she asked, concerned at the bleak look on his face.

"I thought you were upstairs," was all he said.

"I had some work to do on the computer."

"Have we heard anything back from Albert Grimmon?"

"We're supposed to meet with him Wednesday."

"Almost a week from now."

"He's gone until Tuesday so that's why."

His only response to this was a curt nod.

She felt a sliver of dread at his aloof attitude. This morning, before he left for his meeting with her father, he had given her a smile and a kiss and the promise of a date tonight.

"How was your meeting with my dad?"

Garret walked over to the chair across the desk and dropped into it, looking past her through the window. "This is a good place," he said, his tone suddenly quiet, ignoring her question. "I've lived everywhere, but since I left the ranch, this is the first place that feels like a home."

"It's always been my second home," she said quietly. "And I'm so thankful that you love it too. That means so much to me."

The melancholy smile that had pulled at Garret's mouth disappeared and as he turned to her, his eyes turned a glacial gray, his frown reappearing.

"What's wrong?" she asked.

Garret pulled his hand over his face again and sat back in his chair. "Nothing. It's just—" He blew out a sigh. "The cash flow thing is frustrating."

Larissa relaxed back against her chair relief sluicing through her. So that was what bothered him. "Once we talk to Albert we'll get a better idea of what's happening," she assured him. "I know we can make this inn profitable. It was once before, I don't know why it can't be again."

"That's the trouble, isn't it? We don't know why."

Larissa felt the chill again, but dismissed it. Garret was simply expressing frustration she'd been feeling, too.

"What are you working on?" he asked.

Thankful for the diversion she glanced back at the computer screen. "I'm just going over some of the bills and receipts from the scrapbooking conference. Orest usually pays all the bills and takes care of invoicing, but I thought I should start finding out for myself how things work." She shrugged. "I'm sort of stumbling along here but from what I can see, we should have made a profit from this conference."

"That's what we said about Pete's conference," Garret ground out. "But that didn't happen either, according to Orest. I'm not sure we can trust—" Garret stopped, pushing himself to his feet and walking to the window behind Larissa's desk.

"You're not sure we can trust him?" Larissa finished Garret's comment, feeling a twist of disloyalty. "Is that why you wanted the external audit?"

Garret nodded slowly, his back to Larissa, his hands shoved deep in the pockets of his suit pants, his coat straining at his broad shoulders. From behind, his hair curled over the collar of his jacket, a dark contrast to the gray of his suit. He rearranged the waves with a quick shove of his hand, then spun around.

"What would you do if you didn't have the inn?"

Larissa swallowed down her trepidation at his question. "What are you trying to say?"

"I'm just curious. You're so tied up in this place, sometimes it feels like I don't know where the inn quits and you begin." He added a smile but it did nothing for Larissa's equilibrium.

"I feel like this place is a part of me," she said quietly. "I think I would lose my identity if I had to leave this place."

"Do you think that's a good thing? To have your identity so tied up in a place?"

Larissa felt her back stiffen, surprised at Garret's questions. "I don't think it's a bad thing. I think we all need to know who we are and what's important to us. I think we all need a sense of place. To feel connected. The inn is my home."

"Not the house you were raised in?" Garret's quirk of his eyebrow told her how silly that might have sounded.

She shook her head. "No. Not the house. That was just a place to sleep. This was where I spent the most time with my mother."

"So is this a business for you, or a way to keep your mother's memory alive?"

Larissa fought down a flicker of disquiet at Garret's almost harsh tone as his questions mirrored her own uncertainties. Was she just holding on to the inn to keep her mother's memory alive as Garret said?

She was afraid to ask because to do so felt as if she was being a traitor to her mother's legacy. Before her mother died, she had asked Larissa to take care of the inn. To make sure it kept going. And she had.

But before she could formulate a response to his rapid-fire questions, Garret made a left to right swipe with his hands as if erasing what he just said. "Sorry. That's an unfair question." He shoved his hand through his hair again and released a long, heavy sigh.

Larissa weighed her thoughts, measured her memories as she struggled to find the right way to say what she needed to say. To not let Garret's questions resurrect the fear that spiraled through her.

"When my mother was dying she asked me to take care of the inn. That's one of the reasons I want to keep this inn going. The other is that it's truly a part of me."

Garret nodded and took a step closer to her. "But when you have to make a business decision, what criteria do you use? Your need to keep your mother's legacy alive, or the reality of where the inn is going?"

"It's doing okay. It has to get better and it will but for now, we're getting by."

Garret released a cynical laugh. "I don't want to just 'get by'," he said. "I've done that enough in my life."

His words made her uncomfortable. She knew that money was important to Garret. Even though he said he didn't take ten thousand dollars from her father, he left because of money and his concern that he couldn't give her enough of it. "Money isn't everything."

"No. It isn't. But try to keep your car on the road without it. Try to put food on the table without it. Try to provide for a family without it." He stopped there, his hands clenched at his side. He released his fists slowly and flexed his fingers.

She heard the rising anger in his voice and it made her pull back. "I know you've had your hardships, Garret. But I also know that this inn isn't just a business to you, either. I've heard how you talk about this place. It means something to you too." She stopped there, not sure she could keep the fear out of her voice. Or the pleading.

Garret blew out a sigh, then walked over to her. "I'm sorry, Larissa." He laid his hand on her shoulder, his fingers lightly caressing her neck. "I don't want us to fight about this."

"I don't either."

He gave her a cautious smile and cupped her chin in his hand, looking into her eyes his own intent, direct, like a laser. "I've got to go away for a while."

She felt a sense of foreboding as he spoke, wondering what happened to the date they were supposed to have tonight. What had come up that he had to cancel?

But pride kept her question unvoiced. Instead, she only nodded. "Sure. When will you be back?"

"I'll stay in touch."

Again, all she could do was nod at his vague comment. He

gave her a quick kiss, which seemed to be more afterthought than a caress. Then he straightened and walked away.

Larissa watched him leave, watched as he walked toward the parking lot. Watched as he started his car and drove away without a second glance backward.

Through the open window Larissa heard the burbling of the creek counterpointed by a robin's cheerful song. She leaned her chin on her cupped hand, waiting for the peace that usually came over her when looking outside.

She thought of all the years she had spent here. Of the changing of the seasons and the plans she had spun and woven around the inn.

She had always imagined that when she got married, it would be here at the inn. She would have a gazebo set up in the large open area just below the patio. She would come in over the bridge, her long white dress trailing behind her. No veil, just a small spray of flowers on one side of her head. Purple orchids and white roses.

She and Alanna had spent hours planning their weddings. The styles of the dress and the colors of the flowers always changed but one thing was constant.

The inn.

At one time she had a clear picture of who would be waiting for her at the end of the aisle. Then, when Garret left, the man was just a blur in a tuxedo.

But lately...lately she dared give the man a face again. A name. Did she still dare?

On the heels of that question, more came tumbling to the fore.

Why was he asking the questions he had about the inn? What was he planning? Why didn't he tell her where he was going and what he was doing?

And, even worse, would he come back?

FIFTEEN

Larissa kept herself busy in the office for the rest of the afternoon. Each time she heard the front door of the inn open, her heart plunged in her chest.

Then the inn door opened again and this time, a few seconds later, her office door creaked open and her father stepped into the room.

He gave her a somber look then closed the door behind him. "Do you have a few moments? I've something I need to tell you."

Larissa's smile froze at the disquiet in his voice. First Garret, now her father? What was going on?

"Sure," she said, shaking off the sense of foreboding. "What do you need to say?"

He didn't reply right away. Instead he stood by the door, looking around the room, a wistful smile tugging at his mouth.

"You and your mother spent a lot of time in this place," he said quietly. "I remember how you used to play here while she was working."

Larissa nodded, remembering how she used to set her dolls

up on the floor by the desk while her mother would pay bills and did all the bookkeeping.

Sometimes Larissa would sit on her mother's lap, and play with the pens and pencils sitting in a cup on the desk. When she grew older, she would do her homework in here. When Larissa started high school, Orest took over the bookkeeping. Then Larissa would help her mother with the housekeeping, supervising the work in the kitchen. Consult with Emily. Help with the ordering.

A wistful smile pulled at Larissa's mouth.

"You know, some of my best memories of Mom weren't at home. They were here. In this inn," Larissa said.

"Your mother's whole life was wrapped up in this inn," her father said. "Many memories, that's for sure."

The pensive note in his voice and his mournful smile gave her heart a nervous flutter. He was talking about the inn as if it was something in the past. Or something that would soon be in the past.

"Why did you want to talk to me?" she asked, threading her now-chilly fingers together, her smile suddenly forced.

"Did Garret come by after our meeting this morning?"

Larissa nodded, her fingers tightening. The ring her mother had given her dug into her skin.

"Did he tell you what we talked about?"

"We didn't talk about your meeting." Which was true. But she wasn't going to mention what Garret had said to her, waiting to hear what her father would say.

"I wanted to come sooner to talk to you about it, but I had other business to take care of at the mill." He released a heavy sigh. "I know this isn't what you want to hear, but Garret and I talked about selling the inn."

For a moment all she could do was stare at her father, his words falling like shards of glass from a broken window. She didn't want to pick them up. To arrange them into something that made sense.

We talked...selling the inn...

Right behind that came an echo of Garret's question.

What would you do if you didn't have the inn?

"What did you and Garret decide?" she asked, disappointed to hear how reedy and weak her voice sounded.

Jack eased out a sigh. "Larissa, you have to be realistic. The inn isn't doing as well as it used to."

"But we just had two successful conferences and the bookings are up. We've got to be making some headway."

Her dad walked over to her and put his hands on her shoulders. His reassuring move was an echo of what had happened another time. When Garret had left before.

She shook the déjà vu off. She was just being silly. Garret hadn't left. He was just...just...

Her mind ticked back to Garret's preoccupation today. She thought it was because of the finances of the inn. But now?

"I know it's not what you want to hear but you know what Orest has been telling us. This isn't working, honey. It's time to let go."

The sorrow on her father's face and threaded through his voice battered at all her insecurities. She didn't want to believe that Garret would simply turn his back on what they had worked so hard to build.

But she couldn't dismiss what her father told her either. And on the heels of that came a memory of when Garret first arrived. How he had talked about the inn's potential. Like it was just another asset. However, she also knew that the inn was not his first choice. That the mill was the prize he'd been gunning for.

Was that what was behind all the questions and now what

her father told her? Was the inn simply a jumping point for Garret? Was it always about the mill?

She shook her head to dislodge the renegade thoughts. She couldn't think here. Couldn't think at all. Too many emotions too many memories.

"I don't think I can be here," she said, her voice breaking.

Her father nodded. "You've been working so hard the past couple of months. Sheila can watch the inn for you. You should take a break. Why don't you just take a couple of days off? I'll let you know what happens."

Maybe she should. Maybe she should get away. Get some perspective. Give herself some room.

So she simply nodded, then gave him a quick kiss and left. No reason to stay here. Garret and her father together owned the majority share of the inn anyway. They didn't need her to make a decision.

She wasn't necessary at all.

When she got home she made a few phone calls, quickly packed her bags and left.

Two hours later she was pulling up to the parking lot of Lydia Porter's bed-and-breakfast. Lydia had been a close friend of her mother's.

She reached for her purse to call her father to tell her where she was and realized that in her rush to leave, she had forgotten her phone back in her office.

No matter. She didn't need to talk to anyone. Didn't need to find out what Garret and her father were planning. She would know soon enough.

She pulled her suitcase out of the car and walked up to the door, her heart sinking in her chest, memories of her mother's friendship with Lydia surfacing. The two of them would travel together and twice a year went down to Mexico for what her mother called her 'spa getaway'.

However, Lydia had just stepped out, but the receptionist knew who Larissa was and quickly escorted her to her room.

Larissa tossed the suitcase on the bed and began unpacking. As she did, she pulled out the Bible she had put in her luggage. She had picked it up from the kitchen counter, where she had left it more than a few weeks ago.

Ever since they started getting ready for Pete's conference.

Guilt weighed on her soul as she lowered herself to the bed, her Bible in her lap. She was quick enough to pray when she wanted something from God.

Lately she hadn't been reading the Bible. The inn had absorbed all her time and had taken over all her waking thoughts.

And the past few weeks...so had Garret.

His voice now sounded in her head. *I don't know where the inn quits and you begin.*

His words crept around the periphery of her mind accompanied by remorse and self-reproach. She had made the inn a huge focus at the cost of her spiritual life. It had kept her busy.

But she wasn't busy now and, if things went the way her father and Garret seemed to be hinting at, she might not be busy like that again.

She subdued the fear that spiraled up her throat and turned her attention to the Bible.

The pages flew through her fingers as she sought some scrap of comfort. Some portion of peace. She turned and turned and then she came to a marked spot.

Matthew 6. Part of the Sermon on the Mount.

Larissa read and then a verse jumped out at her. A verse so familiar, so well-known, her eyes almost slipped over it without letting its words register. Then one word caught her attention. Treasure.

She read, *"Do not store up for yourselves treasures on earth where moths and vermin destroy."* She stopped there, thinking about the work that had to be done on the inn yet. The slow deterioration of a place that she treasured so much. She eased out a weary smile and carried on. *"But store up for yourselves treasures in heaven where moths and vermin do not destroy and where thieves do not break in and steal. For where your treasure is, there your heart will be also."*

She lowered the Bible, letting it rest on her lap as the words slowly seeped into her mind, bringing out other emotions. Had she really made the inn more important in her life than God? Had she really made it her treasure? Had she tried to find her worth in that place instead of in her Lord?

Still holding the Bible open on her lap, she let her thoughts go to a place she had never dared travel.

What would her life be without the inn? As she had told Garret it had been so woven in her life she couldn't see herself apart from it.

But it wasn't making money.

She thought of Garret's comment about trying to provide for a family without money. Was he talking about their future? Or about his past?

She looked back down at the passage. Maybe she had made the inn too much of her "treasure." Maybe she needed to learn to let go. What was more important? Her promise to her mother? Her changing feelings for Garret? Or her relationship with God?

She lowered her head, pressing her hands against her face. *Help me to let go of the things I need to let go of, Lord. Help me to trust in You. Help me store up treasures in heaven. With You. And be with Garret. Watch over him. Keep him safe.* She wasn't sure what else to pray for.

She sat a moment, but then felt restless and headed downstairs. Lydia was still gone so Larissa went into the room often referred to as the library. It was more of a sitting room and a tiny one at that, just off the dining room. A row of shelves lined one wall holding a variety of books that, Larissa was sure, hadn't changed since she was a kid.

She and her mother would visit here from time to time and Larissa always liked checking the bookshelves in the hope that she would find something to pique her interest.

But the room was in an uproar. Books lay in piles on the floor and on the two small tables that flanked a couple of easy chairs. The chairs were also stacked with books. Obviously Lydia thought it was time for an update. Larissa smiled as she walked through the room, noticing books that she remembered reading as a young girl when her mother would come to visit Lydia.

She ran her fingers along the piles on the table, then, as she turned, noticed a number of older photo albums lying in one corner of the room.

She walked over, knelt down and picked one up and flipped it open. Her heart stuttered when she saw her mother smiling out of a picture, her arm flung around Lydia's shoulders. The palm trees in the background, the line of breaking surf behind them and the turquoise of the water clearly showed Larissa this was not Rockyview.

Her mother wore capris, a bathing suit and the largest sun hat Larissa had ever seen. Probably one of their trips to Mexico, Larissa thought as she sat down on the floor, the album in her lap. She paged past a few more touristy photos—beach pictures, snorkeling and shopping photos.

The photos brought a smile to her lips and a gentle sorrow to her heart. Her mother was so happy. So healthy in these pictures. Larissa checked the dates on the photos, four years before her mother died.

She flipped through the album and then, puzzled, stopped

at one of the pages. Her mother was wearing what looked like a hospital gown. An IV was attached to her arm. She sat on the edge of a bed and frowned at the camera, holding her hand up as if in warning.

Had she injured herself on this trip? Larissa couldn't remember her mother talking about being in a hospital.

Larissa looked more closely at the picture. The room her mother was in looked more like a resort than any hospital Larissa had ever been in.

What was going on?

"Hey, honey, heard you were here," Lydia's cheerful voice called out as she entered the room.

Larissa looked up at her mother's friend. Tall, slender and perpetually young-looking with her highlighted blond hair and tanned skin, Lydia never seemed to age.

"Just got here about forty minutes ago," Larissa said, slowly getting to her feet, still holding the photo album. "I see you're doing some changes in here."

Lydia nodded, but when her eyes dropped to the book Larissa held, her smile drifted away. "Where did you find that?" she asked.

The faint note of panic in her voice only added to Larissa's confusion.

"Just lying here on the floor," Larissa said, feeling a beat of guilt. But another glance at the puzzling picture pushed that away. She held up the book, showing Lydia the picture.

"So, what's happening here? Why is my mother in the hospital? What happened to her? Did she get sick on one of your trips?"

Lydia pressed the back of her hand to her mouth, then slowly lowered herself to the edge of the couch. She sighed lightly and gave Larissa a careful smile.

"You weren't supposed to see that picture."

"When was it taken?"

"About eight years ago. Shortly after your mother was diagnosed."

"Did she have some kind of attack?"

Lydia eased out another sigh as she held her hand out for the album. "No. She didn't. She was there on purpose."

Larissa's puzzlement only grew with each thing Lydia said.

"What happened in Mexico, Lydia? What aren't you telling me?"

Lydia cleared away some of the books beside her and patted the empty spot. "Sit down, my dear. I need to tell you something very important."

NANA SAT BACK in her chair, her hands folded over one another. "What do you think you should do?" she asked, her voice quiet, calm.

Garret leaned forward on Nana's couch, his elbows resting on his knees, his chin settled on his hands. He looked over at his grandmother and the gentle smile playing over her lips.

"I don't know. That's why I came here."

When Garret left the inn, he had stopped at his apartment, packed a suitcase and was going to drive to Calgary. He had called his financial adviser who asked him to please come and talk to him before he made any rash decisions.

But even before he went to Calgary, he wanted to make another, more important stop. Nana Bond's place.

All his life Nana had been the voice of sanity and reason in his life. She had been his guiding light, his conscience and spiritual beacon.

Right now he needed all the above to make the right decision.

"I'm going to ask the obvious, but have you prayed about this?"

"I don't know what I want, so how can I pray?"

"God isn't a vending machine," his nana said, her voice holding a gentle note of reprimand. "Prayer is not a matter of choosing what you want and then putting in your request. God wants us to communicate with Him, have a relationship," his grandmother continued. "Not so He can give us what we want, but so that in the praying we acknowledge where our hope really lies. And right now I'm thinking that part of that hope is wound up in Larissa Weir."

Garret released a dry chuckle. "A lot of that hope is wound up in her. I love her."

"I'm happy to hear that," Nana said. "But I'm not sure why that's a problem."

Garret looked over at his grandmother who sat back in her easy chair, her hand resting on the arms, her blue eyes holding his intently.

"Because she wants so badly to keep the inn and I know it can't support us."

"I thought things were going well. You were getting busier."

"I thought so too but the numbers don't look good. At least according to Orest."

"You sound skeptical."

"I don't trust the guy. I'm so sure the inn can turn a profit, but he's completely in charge of the bookkeeping."

"Weren't you getting an audit done by Albert?"

"We're supposed to get the results back from him next week."

"So why don't you wait until then?"

"Because Jack Weir wants to buy my share of the inn and he wants to close the deal before we see Albert."

"I understand." She tapped her fingers. "What do you want to do?"

Garret sighed as his mind shifted back to the conversation he'd just had with Larissa. It was unsatisfying and he'd walked away not sure he'd said or done the right things.

"I want to be with Larissa, but I want to support her. To take care of her. But I also want to make her happy. "

"And you think that means keeping the inn?"

"I think it's what she thinks. But in order to do that, in order to keep the inn going, I have to sell my investments and plow that money into the inn. And right now is not a good time to sell. I'll get almost half of what I put in. And I'm not sure it will help."

His grandmother sighed, then got up and walked over to his side, settling beside him on the couch. She put her arm over his shoulders, like she used to when he was much younger and much smaller. She had to reach up to do it now, though.

"It's just money, Garret."

"But I worked so hard to get it together," he said.

"Did you do it all by yourself?"

Garret felt the faint rebuke in her voice and he knew she was right. While they were growing up his grandparents had always told him that money was a gift and a tool given to them by God. He had heard it but it had never really sunk in. Until now.

"Wouldn't I be a poor steward if I simply threw good money after bad?" he asked.

"I keep hearing you say that you feel the inn can make you a living. It wouldn't be poor stewardship if your money could make the difference."

"Even if I do that, I don't know if it's enough to support Larissa. She's been getting money from her grandparent's estate. That's the only way she's been able to live off what the inn makes."

"Do you know how much it is? Because from the way she lives, I don't think she's spending a lot of money. Her car isn't exactly top of the line and I never see her in fancy clothes or shoes."

"I never paid that much attention to the quality of Larissa's clothes," Garret said.

"Of course not. You've been distracted by other things," his nana said with a smile. Then she took Garret's hand in hers. "I think you know what you want to do. And right now, I think you need to let go of the idea that Larissa needs to live a certain way in order for her to be happy. If she really loves you, then it won't matter how much money you have or don't have. How much money you make or don't make," she said, a stern note in her voice. "Right now I think you're more concerned about the money than she is."

Garret nodded, acknowledging the rightness of his grandmother's comment, so similar to Shannon's awhile back.

"So. We need to take care of one thing first," his grandmother said, giving his hand a light shake. "We're going to pray together and then you're going to go talk to your money guy. On the drive to Calgary I'm sure you'll discover what needs to happen."

Garret looked over at his grandmother and smiled at her. "You're a blessing to me, you know?"

"I try to be," she returned with a smile. "And you've always been a blessing to me, too."

Then she covered his other hand with hers and together they bowed their heads and put everything before the Lord.

TWO DAYS later Garret pulled up to the front of the inn. He'd spent the past few days getting everything in order and trying to phone Larissa. But she wasn't at the inn and she wasn't answering her cell phone.

He'd gone through all sorts of indecision as he tried to contact her, but in the end he knew what he wanted to do, not only for Larissa, but also for himself.

He walked up the walk, ignoring the windows on the upper floor that needed replacing and the faint sag in the veranda.

All in good time.

He pulled open the door of the inn, feeling a sense of coming home. It made him smile and it gave him the encouragement he needed to do what he had to do.

Thank you, Lord, he prayed as he looked around the lobby of the inn. Sheila looked up at him and waved. He returned her greeting, then walked over to the office door and opened it. On the way he had called and told Jack he would meet him here at the inn.

Garret stifled a jolt of regret as he stepped into the office and saw only Jack behind the desk. Though he had arranged this meeting between him and Jack, a small part of him had hoped Larissa would be there as well.

Still gone. He tried not to get panicky about her lack of communication.

Jack leaned back in his chair, his steepled fingers under his chin. "So, I'm assuming your little trip away from here was to help you make a decision?"

Garret nodded and dropped into a chair across from Jack. "Yes. I had to talk to my financial adviser."

"And what did he tell you?"

"Before we talk about that, I want to know where Larissa is."

Jack rocked a moment in his chair. "She needed a break.

Too many things happening too quickly." Then he leveled him a serious look. "Why should I tell you that?"

Garret felt it again. That old feeling of unworthiness. But then he remembered how Jack had kept him and Larissa apart the first time and he knew he wouldn't be intimidated by this man again. "I love your daughter and I'm doing right by her this time. I'm not giving in to you. I'm not selling my shares of the inn to you. I know that you'll turn around and sell the inn anyway, but not before you break off a few parcels of the land to subdivide it."

Jack frowned. "How did you know that?"

"Pete Boonstra told me. Actually he dropped it in passing as I was talking to him yesterday about the real value of the inn."

"And you needed to know that value because..." Jack frowned at him, waiting.

"Because I'm buying your shares of the inn instead."

"Why would you want to do that? You know what the financials are and I know that you are a savvy businessman. I know you didn't make your money by making poor business decisions." Jack rubbed his temple with a forefinger, looking suddenly weary. "I've been trying to tell Larissa to let go of this inn for years, but she won't." He blew out his breath. "It will suck the life out of both of you, like it did out of my wife. And it won't make you the money you're used to as an engineer."

"You're right. It won't, but you know, I've learned a few things along the way. To me buying this inn isn't about choosing money. It's about choosing to be with the woman I love and to be involved in what she loves. At all costs."

"Do you think you can give Larissa what she wants this time around?"

Garret hesitated, sending up another prayer for wisdom, for patience and for strength.

"I don't think Larissa is the girl she used to be and I'm not the man I used to be. But I'm leaving the decision up to Larissa. I'm not assuming what she needs anymore. I'm letting her make up her own mind about what will happen. Whatever she wants to do with this inn, I'll stand by her. I love her more than I ever thought I could love someone and I believe that covers a lot. I believe, with God's help, we can make this relationship work."

Jack looked him in the eye and shrugged. "Maybe you can," he returned. Then he looked over Garret's shoulder.

Garret felt a prickling at the back of his neck. When he turned around he saw Larissa standing in the doorway, a suitcase at her feet, her hand over her mouth. From the look in her eyes, he guessed she had heard some of what he said.

His heart turned over in his chest and he walked to her side and took her hands in his. "I've been wanting to talk to you for the past two days."

"I left my cell phone here. In the office," she said, her voice quiet. Then she shook her head, her bright eyes holding his. "That's not what I wanted to say."

"Let's go somewhere else to talk." He took her arm and led her away from the office and away from her father. They walked out the front door in silence to the bridge over the creek.

He stopped there, still holding her hand, still trying to absorb the fact that she was here. That she had heard the declaration he had wanted to make to her face.

The river burbled beneath their feet, the steady flow of water reminding Garret of the flow of their lives as he clung to her hand. He and Larissa had been through a lot to get here and he wasn't letting her go.

He reached up and stroked a strand of hair away from her face. "I missed you," he said quietly.

"Where did you go?"

"I had some important business to take care of." He took a chance and brushed a kiss over her forehead. Then she leaned against him, wrapping her arms around him.

"I heard what you said to my father."

"About the inn?" he said, deliberately misunderstanding her.

"That and the rest," she said with a gentle smile.

Garret let his fingers drift over her beloved face, his eyes following the path of his hand, noting the changes that had happened during the intervening years. "I do love you, you know. I always have," he said, as he traced the curve of her lips, the line of her jaw.

She caught his hand and pressed a kiss to his palm, holding his gaze, her own steadfast. "I've always loved you too. I never stopped thinking about you, wishing things had gone differently—"

He touched a finger to her lips to stop whatever else she might say. "Whatever happened, happened for a reason. I sincerely believe God had better things in mind for us. Maybe we both needed to learn some hard lessons. I know I did."

"What lessons did you need to learn?" she asked, her tone puzzled.

He was quiet a moment, still uncertain how much she would understand. But if they were going to move ahead, he knew he had to be honest with her. "I needed to learn what really matters. That money doesn't give you freedom or power in spite of what I had seen. I needed to learn that money is a gift from God and that we are entrusted with it. And I needed to learn that when you went against your father's wishes, I knew that I could trust you completely."

Larissa stood up on her toes and pressed a kiss to his lips. He returned it and for a few blissful moments all was forgotten. The only people who existed in this world were the two of them, here in this place that had created a sense of home and belonging.

Then Larissa let her hand rest on his shoulder, her expression suddenly serious.

"What's wrong?" he asked, twisting a strand of her hair around his finger.

Larissa pulled back, giving him a plaintive smile. "I left after you did to stay at a bed-and-breakfast that a friend of my mother runs. They were very close. For the last four years of my mother's life they would go together to Mexico. For a break, my mother always said." She stopped there, pressing her lips together as she shook her head.

"What's wrong?" he asked quietly.

She drew in a slow breath. "I always thought it was a holiday. But while I was staying at Lydia's B&B I saw some photo albums from one of their trips. Lydia had been looking at it before I came and had forgotten about it. Apparently I wasn't supposed to see it. In the album I saw a picture of my mother sitting on what looked like a hospital bed. I asked Lydia what that was about and very reluctantly she told me the truth about the trips she and my mother made to Mexico. It was for alternative treatments for my mother's cancer. Treatments that were very experimental and very expensive."

She stopped and Garret felt as if pieces of a puzzle were slowly falling into place.

"Did she ever tell you about them?"

She shook her head. "Apparently not even my father knew. Lydia said he would have talked her out of doing them. So I called Orest and asked him if he knew. After much sighing and hemming and hawing he told me that the treatments had been so expensive my mother had taken out a loan she didn't want my father knowing about." Larissa's voice broke and she stopped there, lowering her hand as if retreating. "That's why the inn couldn't make any money. Orest was juggling accounts trying to pay the loan without making it look like he was paying it."

"So he wasn't taking money." Garret felt a moment of shame that he had practically accused the older man of stealing, but what else could he have thought?

"No. But he was covering for my mother's mistakes."

Sensing her shame and the echoes of older pain and loss, Garret drew her close. "It doesn't matter. Not now."

"Yes, it does," Larissa mumbled against his chest. "Why didn't she tell me about the treatments? Or my father? How could she be so selfish and not think we should be involved?"

"I don't think she was being selfish," Garret said. He swallowed down his own flicker of sorrow. "I remember how much my mother cried when she thought she wouldn't see me and Tanner grow up. I'm sure your mother felt the same way. I'm sure she hoped that what she did was an investment in the future. A future with you and your father."

Larissa was quiet a moment, then she looked up at him, her eyes shimmering with the remnants of her tears. "Thank you for that," she whispered.

Garret kissed her again. "You're welcome." He smiled down at her, then reached into his pocket, wanting to move the conversation to a happier topic. "And speaking of investments..."

He pulled out the necklace and let it dangle from his finger.

She frowned when she saw the gold nugget at the end of the chain catching the sunlight, throwing it back at her.

"Is that one of the necklaces your grandmother had made out of the nuggets?"

Garret nodded. "Hailey, Shannon, and Naomi all wear theirs. But Tanner gave his to Sabine." Then he carefully slipped the necklace over Larissa's head. "And I'm giving mine to you. It's my way of saying that I want you in my life. That I choose you just like August chose Nukinu. That I'm willing to do whatever it takes to keep us together."

Larissa fingered the gold nugget, a lone tear trickling down her cheek as she did. "I...I don't know what to say."

"You don't need to say anything. Just nod. Or, if you don't accept, you can just turn and walk away."

Larissa turned her face up to his, "Of course I accept. You've always been the only one I wanted to spend the rest of my life with."

Garret smiled, gave her another kiss and slipped his arm around her shoulder. "With or without the inn?"

"With or without the inn," she agreed. "I know the inn was too important to me. Too much a legacy from my mother. I put it in the wrong place in my life. I learned that in the past few days. So if you think you should sell your share to my father, or if you want to sell it to someone else, then that's fine."

"I thought you said you heard everything I said to your father."

"I know, but it isn't necessary."

"But it is. Because this inn was a place of healing for me," he said quietly, his fingers caressing her shoulder. "It's a place where I realized the importance of legacy and community. And now that I know about the loan, I'm even more determined to make a go of this place." He paused, in spite of his brave words, still feeling the remnants of faint panic clawing at him. "I've cashed in my investments. I'm using that money to buy out your father and now that I know why the inn hasn't been making money, I'm sure we'll be able to make a profit."

Larissa gave him a wistful smile. "Paying out that loan won't be as hard as you think. Apparently my mother had also used my grandparent's legacy to pay for some of the treatments. Money that was supposed to come to me. To protect her secret,

Orest paid me from the income of the inn, even though the inheritance was all used up by my mother."

"Your father told me about that money," Garret said, lowering his arm. "He said that you were able to supplement the income you got from the inn with that."

Larissa's laughter was a surprise to him. "I didn't supplement my income at all. Every penny I got from that inheritance was put into a savings account. I was hoping to use it to eventually buy out my father. It wasn't enough for that, but it is enough to do some of the renovations I wanted to do in the first place."

Garret was surprised at the relief he felt at her declaration. "So all along, you've been getting by on what you've been drawing from the inn?"

"Of course," she said, sounding surprised. "More than getting by." Then she gave him a mischievous grin, as if she knew what he was thinking. "And you know exactly how much that amount is. I'm not the spoiled high-maintenance girl you seem to think I am."

"Never spoiled and never high-maintenance," he said, with a touch of shame.

"But you did think that at one time."

"I was an idiot at one time," he returned. "But I know you better now and I know myself better now. I'd like to think we've both grown up. I know I've had to learn where to store up my treasure."

Larissa smiled at him. "I have, too. And I am praying that together we can help each other trust in God as well as each other."

"I'm praying the same thing," he said with a gentle smile. He pressed a kiss to her lips, then brushed her hair away from her face and slipped his arm around her, and looked out over the property. "This is a good place," he said. "I think we'll do well here."

"I know we will," she said, tucking herself against his side. "Mostly because we'll be working on it together."

"I like the sound of that," he said, pulling her close.

She sighed a little, then drew back to hold his gaze. "So you won't regret not buying the mill? You have as much of a chance to get it as my father, right?"

Garret heard the uncertainty in her voice and shook his head. "No. I won't regret it at all." He looked past her at the trees sheltering the creek and the grass rolling away toward the inn, so settled into the landscape. "The mill can never give me what this inn can."

"And what is that?"

"All the cake and pie I can eat and a place for my cousins to have their weddings," he joked.

They laughed, but then he grew serious as his fingers drifted over her beloved features. "The mill is a business, but this place is a way of life. A vocation if you will. Something that we can do together. Which means more to me than any income the mill could generate."

Larissa's smile shone brighter than the sun overhead. He kissed her again and caught her by the arm. "We should be getting back before your father leaves," he said. "I have something I need to talk to him about."

Larissa tilted her head to one side. "And what would that be?"

"We need to resolve some of the business stuff. About me taking over the inn."

Her hopeful expression faded a little but then she rallied with a quick smile. "Of course."

"And I need to take care of a little detail about my plans for his daughter's future," he added.

Larissa grinned up at him. "I see," was all she said.

He held out his arm to her and she tucked hers into it.

"Shall we do this together?" he asked.

"I think that's a great idea."

He took her arm in his and this time they walked back to the inn, their footsteps reverberating on the wooden bridge, a faint echo from their past life.

He paused at the end of the bridge, then looked around at the grounds of the inn. "You know, you always had the right idea."

"What do you mean?"

He turned to her and brushed a strand of hair away from her face. "I think this inn is the perfect place for a wedding."

Larissa's only response was to step up on her tiptoes and give him a gentle kiss.

Garret held her close, feeling as if his life had come full circle to this amazing, wonderful place. As if all the struggles they had both gone through, the choices they made were now vindicated.

Then he took her hand, gave it a light squeeze and a gentle smile, and he thanked God that they were now, finally, reunited again.

REMEMBER NAOMI? Shannon and Hailey's sister who was in Halifax? Well, she came home and here's a teaser of her story:

FINDING HOME

It wasn't supposed to happen this soon. She wasn't supposed to see him yet. She wasn't ready.

Naomi ran her suddenly damp palms over her apron. She grabbed the tray of fresh-baked brownies and slipped them into the display case of Mug Shots, the café she worked at part-time. Then she straightened and looked directly into the eyes of Jess Schroder and the part of her past she spent years trying to keep buried.

Good-looking as ever, she thought, her heart doing the same silly flip it always did whenever she saw him all those years ago. Time had filled out his broad shoulders, narrowed his waist, lent interesting shadows and hollows to his handsome features. He still wore his hair a little long and it still waved over his forehead and into his eyes, but it had darkened from the blond it used to be to a light brown. His square jaw was shadowed by stubble, narrow nose, chiseled features and dark eyes that seemed to drill into her very soul.

"What can I get you?" she asked, pleased that her voice could sound so casual.

He shot her a frown, as if surprised that she didn't swoon at his feet. Like she almost did every day that summer she tutored him.

That summer they dated.

"Hey, Naomi," he said quietly, slipping his hand in the back pocket of his blue jeans. "I heard you were back in town."

His deep voice tugged at memories she thought had been lost in the onslaught of what had happened since that summer they spent together ten years ago.

Please, Lord, help me through this. Help me to stay focused on You.

Her prayer was a cry from a wounded heart still struggling after her fiancé's death. From the move back from a place she had lived for the past ten years. Moving from Halifax had been difficult but after Billy's death, she needed to come back to her family. Especially now that all her cousins were settled back in Rockyview.

Nursing Billy the past few months of his life had been

wrenching, difficult but she never once regretted the time she had spent with him.

She knew when she came back to Rockyview she would be seeing Jess again. She thought she had prepared herself for it.

But from the way her heart hammered in her chest, guess not.

She drew in another long breath, then another and thankfully, she felt her equilibrium return.

"I got back a few weeks ago," she said, thankful that her feelings didn't seep into her voice.

Jess's expression grew suddenly serious. "I heard about Billy. I was sorry to hear about his death."

Before she could acknowledge his sympathy, the door of the café opened again and an unfamiliar young girl, obviously pregnant, came inside and waddled over to Jess's side. "So, Jess, you buying me lunch?" she asked. The girl eased out a sigh as she pushed her black hair away from her face.

Naomi glanced from Jess to the girl who didn't look a day over sixteen and then at her protruding stomach. Her emotions spun again as she tried to reconcile the girl's age with the man standing in front of her.

The man who had once held her heart.

YOU CAN GET Finding Home by visiting Amazon and searching for Finding Home by Carolyne Aarsen

If you enjoyed the book Coming Home, it would be awesome if you could leave a review.

Reviews help other readers find my books and help me to keep writing! Knowing my stories made a connection with my readers warms my heart and keeps the fingers flying over the keyboard making more stories.

Blessings to you!

OTHER SERIES

FAMILY BONDS

#1 SEEKING HOME

A rancher who suffered a tragic loss. A single mother on the edge. Can these two find the courage to face a romantic new beginning?

#2 CHOOSING HOME

If you like emergency room drama, second chances, and quaint small-town settings, then you'll adore this romance.

#3 COMING HOME

He thought she chose a hotel over him. She thought he loved money more than her. Years later, can they fill the emptiness in their hearts?

#4 FINDING HOME

She's hiding a terrible truth. He's trying to overcome his scandalous history. Together, forgiveness might give them a second chance.

FAMILY TIES

Four siblings trying to finding their way back to family and faith

A COWBOY'S REUNION

He's still reeling from the breakup. She's ashamed of what she did. Can a chance reunion mend the fence, or are some hearts forever broken? If you like second chance stories, buried passions, and big country settings, then you'll love this emotional novel.

"I enjoyed this book and had trouble putting it down and had to finish it. If the rest of this series is this

great, I look forward to reading more books by Carolyne Aarsen." Karen Semones - Amazon Review

THE COWBOY'S FAMILY

She's desperate. He's loyal. Will a dark lie hold them back from finding love on the ranch? If you like determined heroines, charming cowboys, and family dramas, then you'll love this heartfelt novel.

"What a wonderful series! The first book is Cowboy's Reunion. Tricia's story begins in that book. Emotional stories with wonderful characters. Looking forward to the rest of the books in this series." Jutzie - Amazon reviewer

TAMING THE COWBOY

A saddle bronc trying to prove himself worthy to a father who never loved him. A wedding planner whose ex-fiancee was too busy chasing his own dreams to think of hers. Two people, completely wrong for each other who yet need each other in ways they never realized. Can they let go of their own plans to find a way to heal together?

"This is the third book in the series and I have loved them all. . . . can't wait to see what happens with the last sibling." - Amazon reviewer

THE COWBOY'S RETURN

The final book in the Family Ties Series:

He enlisted in the military, leaving his one true love behind.

She gave herself to a lesser man and paid a terrible price.

In their hometown of Rockyview, they can choose to come together or say a final goodbye...

'This author did an amazing job of turning heartache into happiness with realism and inspirational feeling."
Marlene - Amazon Reviewer

SWEETHEARTS OF SWEET CREEK

Come back to faith and love

#1 HOMECOMING

Be swept away by this sweet romance of a woman's search for belonging and second chances and the rugged rancher who helps her heal.

#2 - HER HEART'S PROMISE

When the man she once loved reveals a hidden truth about the past, Nadine has to choose between justice and love.

#3 - CLOSE TO HIS HEART

Can love triumph over tragedy?

#4 - DIVIDED HEARTS

To embrace a second chance at love, they'll need to discover the truths of the past and the possibilities of the future...

#5 - A HERO AT HEART

If you like rekindled chemistry, family drama, and small, beautiful towns, then you'll love this story of heart and heroism.

#6 - A MOTHER'S HEART

If you like matchmaking daughters, heartfelt stories of mending broken homes, and fixer-upper romance, then this story of second chances is just right for you.

HOLMES CROSSING SERIES

The Only Best Place is the first book in the Holmes Crossing Series.

#1 THE ONLY BEST PLACE

One mistake jeopardized their relationship. Will surrendering her dreams to save their marriage destroy her?

#2 ALL IN ONE PLACE

She has sass, spunk and a haunting secret.

#3 THIS PLACE

Her secret could destroy their second chance at love

#4 A SILENCE IN THE HEART

Can a little boy, an injured kitten and a concerned vet with his own past pain, break down the walls of Tracy's heart?

#5 ANY MAN OF MINE

Living with three brothers has made Danielle tired of guys and cowboys. She wants a man. But is she making the right choice?

#6 A PLACE IN HER HEART

Her new boss shattered her dreams and now she has to work with him. But his vision for the magazine she loves puts them at odds. Can they find a way to work together or will his past bitterness blind him to future love.

.

Made in the USA
Monee, IL
15 January 2023

25342449R20125